KEEP ME

A PHOENIX NOVEL

STACEY KENNEDY

For everyone who has faced their fears for love.

Stacey Kennedy

www.staceykennedy.com

Edited by Lexi Smail

Copy Edited by Monica Bogza

Cover Design by Regina Wamba

Manufactured in Canada

PROLOGUE

"You failed to keep your promise," Archer Westbrook said, sliding onto the metal chair in the West Village coffee shop.

Opposite him, Wayne Newton, a twenty-something, thin-as-a-rail hacker from Brooklyn, sank down in his seat. He pushed his round glasses up his nose, his dark eyes wary. "Listen, it's not my fault."

"Not your fault?" Archer's jaw muscles twitched as he leaned across the bistro table, the aromatic scent of espresso infusing the air in the shop. "You swore your firewalls were unhackable." Firewalls Wayne was paid six figures a year to create and monitor to ensure the personal information of the members of Phoenix, a sex club that catered to the elite of New York City society, were kept safe and private. "But someone broke into our system last night." And that breach had gotten someone inside the club, someone who did not belong there, putting all Phoenix members at risk. Members who paid hundreds of thousands of dollars a year to ensure their voyeuristic, erotic lifestyle remained out of the public eye. As head of security at Phoenix, the breach landed heavily on Archer's shoulders. "Explain to me how that happened."

"Elise Fanning," Wayne said, keeping his voice soft regardless of the grinding of the coffee and the loud chatter surrounding them.

Ready to fire this kid, who'd come highly recommended by more than one person in the security industry, Archer lifted an eyebrow. "Should I know that name?"

"She's a private investigator," Wayne reported, shrinking down farther into his chair at whatever crossed Archer's expression, looking ready to run. "She lives in Brooklyn but works here in Manhattan. This breach leads back to her."

Archer leaned in farther, gritting his teeth. He had fought in wars, carried out top-secret missions with the United States Special Forces, and he never failed. Not like this. A breach of this magnitude was inexcusable. "Is she capable of hacking the system you implemented?"

Wayne looked aghast. "Hell no, man."

"Then, what? She outsourced this?"

Shoulders curling, Wayne waited for a couple to walk past the table before he answered. "I'll have to look into that before I have a concrete answer for you." His hand shook as he took a quick sip of his frappuccino. "But all I know is she couldn't have gotten through my system. This is expert-level shit."

Archer had assumed as much, but he didn't like fuck-ups either, and he wouldn't let Wayne off the hook. "Are there fingerprints, markers in the code, anything that indicates who got past you?"

"No, man. Nothing. Whoever got through left nothing, but I'll find them. There are only so many places they can hide."

"Do it swiftly," Archer demanded, rising and purposely towering over the kid. "Clean this up. Get the system back in order and amp up the security, or your contract is terminated. All clear?"

Wayne stopped blinking, maybe even breathing. "Yes. Yes. Got it. I'll get this all fixed."

"See to it," Archer shot back. "And get me everything you can on Elise Fanning."

"Everything?" Wayne asked.

Archer let his anger show on his face, pressed his knuckles into the table, and loomed over Wayne. "What she eats. When she eats. What she sleeps in. Who she fucks. I want to know every single thing about her. But most importantly, I want to know if she's a danger to us."

TWO MONTHS LATER

"*I*'ll take an Old Forester on the rocks," Archer said to the bartender of the classy New York City cigar lounge.

Fitz, a long-time employee of the cigar lounge, smiled. "Coming right up." He looked plucked from a different era with his handlebar mustache curling up at the ends and his wise, amber-colored eyes.

The cigar lounge was full of customers tonight, sitting at the round tables, enjoying fine alcohol, ice clinking against their glasses. Smoke billowed from the table next to Archer as the customer lit his cigar, infusing the air with an aroma of burnt coffee and a hint of cinnamon. Soft jazz played from the speakers set high on the walls around the room. Three bartenders dressed in tuxes served up drinks while waiters tended to the customers at the tables. Back when the cigar lounge had been constructed in the 1920s, this spot was a gentleman's club. Now the lounge was a local hotspot. But what was truly special about this building was beneath the shiny hardwood floors. Phoenix, the ultra-exclusive, upscale sex club, only accessible through tunnels once used to bootleg whiskey into the club. Each member was able to request one sex show per month—sex acts, participants, every little detail was of the member's preference, something both Archer and Fitz were long-time participants in. All the members were put through a government-level vetting process before they gained access to Phoenix.

As Fitz fetched Archer's drink, the cigar lounge's door opened and Archer was immediately drawn to the woman in the tight jeans, high heels, and black blouse that showed an enticing hint of cleavage. He had fought in elite missions during his time in the United States Army Special Forces. He knew how to plan a dangerous mission and execute it with flawless precision. But the woman before him, with her long dark-brown hair—that just reached her heart-shaped ass—and sharp dark chocolate-colored brown eyes made his head spin. Elise Fanning, the sexiest, most irritating woman he'd ever met in his twenty-nine years.

When he'd first learned her name from Wayne after she hacked into Phoenix's security, he took the breach personally. Until he found out the reason why she'd broken through his firewall. Elise's best friend, Zoey Parker, had needed to gain membership to confront two members who had wronged her. If it had been Archer's choice, Zoey would have been banned from Phoenix immediately. As it was, Rhys Harrington, Phoenix's owner, felt a connection to Zoey. A connection that had led to their engagement last week.

In the weeks that followed the hacking, security had been stepped up to ensure no one slid past Phoenix's defenses again. But since the security breach, Zoey had seamlessly blended her friends with Rhys', and that meant Archer had gotten to know Elise on a personal level. First, she had gotten under his skin with her sass and snark and her ability to outsmart him at every turn, including finding a way past his security. Then she got into his head by being the most curious creature he'd ever met. He wanted to peel back all her layers until he had her naked, exposed—emotionally and physically—and begging for his mouth all over her lush body.

"Anything else for tonight?"

He snapped his eyes back to Fitz and shook his head. "No, thank you."

Fitz's mouth curved at the corner, his gaze flicking to Elise. "A sweet little thing catch your eye?"

"Ha! Sweet?" Archer took a long sip of the bourbon in his glass, catching the spicy notes in the dark amber-colored liquor. "That woman is many things, but sweet is not among them." Cutthroat, wicked smart, and in possession of bigger balls than some men Archer knew.

Fitz chuckled.

Archer's eyes stayed locked on an approaching Elise. Two months ago, Archer would never have believed they were a good match. She couldn't stand him, and he couldn't stand that she'd somehow broken through security he thought unbreakable. But damn, she was fiery and smart and sexy, and his cock hardened in mere seconds of being around her. A reaction she apparently shared as a slight color rose to her cheeks under his watchful stare. "Good evening, Elise," he said when she reached him.

She met him with dark eyes that had the power to freeze him where he stood. "Hello, Archer."

A shudder ran through him at his name on her tongue. Being the center of this woman's attention meant something, demanded a man take notice. "Thank you for coming to see me tonight," he said.

"No problem," she said, sliding onto the stool next to him, facing him. "I'll take a Jim Beam, neat," she said to Fitz. Soft voices drifted over from the table behind them while she watched him with those soul-penetrating eyes that leveled his defenses. Once Fitz delivered her drink and headed off to serve another customer, she added, "I've got to admit, I was surprised that you called me."

"I've got a problem," he told her.

Elise flashed a wicked grin. "A subscription to a women's magazine problem?"

He restrained himself from rolling his eyes. A few days ago, Wayne had delivered a final report on Elise, including details he got off her personal computer. When she discovered her computer had been hacked and Archer was the one behind it, she reciprocated by signing him up for dozens of women's magazine subscriptions. Getting out of those subscriptions had been nothing less than a giant pain in his ass. Four of them were still outstanding, and Archer, for his pride alone, had given in to paying them instead of fighting his way out of the subscriptions. And yet...*and yet*, while they might have come to a truce, and even if it irritated him, she'd impressed him. Not that he'd tell her that. "No, in fact, that problem has been handled," he replied dryly.

She laughed easily, like she didn't have a care in the world. Her long, spectacular legs crossed. "All right, I give. What's the problem?"

"I've got a person I'd like investigated. I need your help."

Her amused expression faltered a moment, surprise glinting in her powerful eyes. "Let me make sure I've got this right. You need *my* help?"

He didn't want to admit it, certainly not to her, but his investigation into her had left only one conclusion: Elise was the best private investigator in the state. Not only did he want to ally himself with her to further protect Phoenix and use her skills to do so, but hiring her gave him a means to get closer to her. "I do, and it requires confidentiality."

Intrigue sparkled in her eyes. "I'm listening. Go on."

"The details are..."—he gestured to all the people around them—"sensitive. Let's take this to my office."

She polished off her drink, then rose. "Lead the way."

He downed the rest of his bourbon and then made his way to the door on the far side, and after he entered in the security code, she followed him inside. The noise from the lounge quieted as he entered his office, which used to be one of the private rooms in the gentleman's club. Old leatherbound books lined the walls surrounding the grand cherrywood desk set near the thin, tall window. Archer skipped his desk and headed for the sitting area with the two brown wingback chairs. He waited for Elise to sit before he joined her and got right to the point. "I've grown suspicious about a member of the club."

"Why? What's happened?" she asked.

"The other night, this person brought her own mask into the club instead of using the ones provided." Every Phoenix member wore a mask. Some, who required their identity hidden, wore full ones. Some demonic and some animalistic. The rest wore simple masquerade masks, being a little more revealing of their identities. "The incident went unnoticed for an hour before one of my security guards picked up on it and we brought her in for questioning."

Elise sat back against her chair, studying him, her expression a well-crafted poker face. "Uh-oh, someone get fired?"

"Suspended for two weeks," he said. His team was composed of retired military who took their failures seriously. Mistakes happened, but they only happened once under Archer's authority. And nothing from the outside was ever allowed inside. Phoenix provided expensive lingerie, masks, anything a member could want. The only exemption were the men's dark slacks, and those were searched methodically for bugs, recording devices, anything that could comprise security. "She brought the mask in a purse that wasn't searched, and that is inexcusable."

Elise watched him for a long moment. "Tell me why this mask worries you."

He rose and moved to his desk, taking out the gold-and-black object in the plastic bag from his locked filing cabinet. "Her behavior was off during questioning," he said, returning to Elise and offering her the mask.

"Off, how?"

"Nervous, edgy." He returned to his seat. "We scanned it for bugs, a camera, anything electronic. We found nothing. I've dug as far as I can go into this member's life, and nothing is showing up that would raise alarms. She said she didn't know the rules about not being able to bring in her own mask, and right now, there's nothing to suggest that's not the truth."

"But your instincts tell you otherwise?"

He nodded, not surprised she'd caught on. Elise's quick mind was what made her stand out. "Everything about this member has me on edge. Something's not right here. I can feel it." He leaned forward, resting his elbows on his knees, leveling her with a measured look. "So, Rhys asked me to extend you an offer. That you investigate this member and that if this job goes well, the club would use your services exclusively going forward." Only because Archer had suggested it to Rhys. Archer was only as good as his team, and Elise had proven herself invaluable.

No wise businessperson would turn down the offer he presented. Phoenix was home to multi-millionaires who paid a pretty penny to stay out of the media. Anyone working in security for the club made a six-figure income, including Archer.

Elise studied him and then the mask. "Can I take this to examine it?"

He nodded. "Of course."

She placed it in her purse before a deep breath spilled

from her pouty lips. "All right, I'll look into this for you. But I need you to do two things for me."

He doubted he was going to like either of the things she wanted. "Name them."

"Get me into the club," she said without a flicker of emotion on her face.

"As a member?" he asked to clarify.

She gave him a flat look. "No, not as a member. I have no interest in watching other people fuck."

Don't knock it until you try it. "For investigatory reasons, then?"

"Exactly," she said with a nod. "Don't tell me the name of this woman or anything about her."

"You don't want to know the name of the woman you're investigating?"

She shook her head. "Let me study the members in person to see if anyone stands out on odd behavior alone." She paused to shrug. "I'm a people reader, and I'm good at it."

He didn't doubt her. She seemed to read straight through him all too easily and knew exactly how to irritate him as much as possible. She was always, in everything she did, one step ahead of him. At first, he'd hated that. He still hated that, but a new sensation burned alongside his annoyance—*desire*. Even now, behind those clever sparkling eyes, he knew she had a plan, a way to manipulate the whole world to her advantage. All he wanted was a single peek into her brilliant mind. "All right, done. And the second request?"

A slow smile filled her face. A hissing kitten would have looked friendlier. "Tell me."

He frowned. "Tell you what?"

"Tell me why you're asking *me* of all people to do this."

Poking his tongue lightly into his cheek, he inhaled deeply. This woman would be the death of him. "Seriously, Elise, you're going to make me say it?"

She gave a firm nod and a wicked grin. "Oh, hell yes, I'm going to make you say it."

"Unbelievable," he muttered, watching her closely. While he did need her help, he needed to level the playing field, so he rose and settled himself in front of her chair. Placing his hands on both armrests, he leaned down. She straightened at his nearness, and her breath hitched when he brought his face down to hers and said, "Elise, you're the best PI out there, and I am desperately in need of your help." He arched an eyebrow, feeling her rapid warm breaths brushing across his face, certain that was lust burning in the depths of her eyes. "Will that suffice?"

Not one to shy away from a game, she rose and slid up against him sensually. "Yes, Archer, that will do. Text me the details when you know what night I'll be coming to the club."

Hard and annoyed that she had the power to even control his damn cock, Archer didn't dare step back. Neither did Elise. "You'll start on this right away?" he asked.

"I've got a current case to wrap up tomorrow morning, but I can begin in the afternoon."

Heat burned in the space between them, drawing him in. "Excellent."

Her gaze swept over his lips before lifting to his eyes again. "We'll talk soon, then."

"We will."

And like the vixen she was, her hand brushed against the front of his pants as she walked away. No doubt she'd felt every inch of his erection. An erection that didn't seem to understand this woman was a complete pain in his ass.

2

"*A*rcher hired you?"

Standing in the galley kitchen of her loft on the southern edge of the Brooklyn Navy Yard, Elise took in the surprise in her roommate and best friend's blue eyes. "Yup, he sure did." She had shared the loft with Hazel Rose since college, and no one knew Elise better. Hazel also knew her tense history with Archer. Even Elise was slightly rattled by his request. She and Archer had been frenemies from day one. She'd beaten him at his own game by breaking through his security, and he wasn't happy about it. That fighting edge had stayed with them whenever they spent time together with Rhys and Zoey. There was this unspoken battle to see who would come out on top. Whether it be winning a bet, beating the other at game night, or eating the most chicken wings, the competitions were endless. But alongside that tension, something else had developed between them. Something hot and needy. And something Elise was having a hard time pushing away. At first, she thought she'd imagined the chemistry between Archer and her. But last night, with a single brush of her hand to confirm, she'd discovered he wanted her as much as she wanted him. And she didn't know what to do with that information. Their thing was butting heads, not screwing.

She reached for her to-go coffee mug from the cupboard, taking a moment to enjoy the warmth from the bright sun shining in through the large windows before turning back to Hazel, who still stared, agape. Elise laughed. "You're about to spill your coffee everywhere."

"Shit!" Hazel rightened the coffeepot. She set it back in the coffee maker, then whirled back to Elise with sparkling eyes. "I take it he's forgiven you for the magazine subscriptions, then?"

"There was nothing to forgive me for," Elise shot back, grabbing the coffeepot and pouring some into her mug. "He's the one who got his hacker to look through my life. I never went that far, even after he pulled that stunt with me. All I did was get Zoey into the club. It was never anything personal, never anything against Archer or Rhys. So what if he had to cancel a few magazine subscriptions—"

"Like ten," Hazel cut in.

Elise rolled her eyes. "Fine, more than a few."

"With each one pissing him off a little bit more."

Elise chuckled and nudged Hazel's shoulder. "Okay, yeah, it did, and maybe I didn't mind getting under his skin." She'd never admit it aloud, but while Archer certainly could rev her engine with all that alpha deliciousness and his seriously good looks, she secretly enjoyed getting past all his defenses. She got the feeling not many people could do that. "But I also didn't take this job for him; I took it for Zoey and Rhys." Because Zoey was the third one in their friendship trio, and Elise was as protective of her friends as she was of her life.

"I'm sure they'll appreciate it too," Hazel said as two bagels popped out of the toaster. Like she did every day,

Hazel slathered the bread in cream cheese and handed one half to Elise. "Are you starting on the case today?"

Elise took a bite of the bagel, then kissed Hazel's cheek. Hazel had always been the "mom" of the trio of friends. She'd been voted "first to get married" and "most likely to have children" in their high school yearbook. All she needed to find was her groom, but neither Elise nor Hazel were successful in that department. "Yup, I'm heading to the office now."

"Stay safe," Hazel called as Elise headed for the door.

"Always do."

She was finished with her bagel by the time she got to the Prospect Park subway stop. It took roughly a half hour to get to Soho by subway. And another ten minutes of walking to arrive at her office in a shared space she rented for an obscene amount of money. Something she would never be able to do if Hazel didn't split rent on the loft.

The security guard, Keith, greeted her with his warm, infectious smile from behind his desk. "Good morning, Miss Elise."

"Morning. I saw the Mets lost last night," Elise said, walking toward the elevators and hitting the button.

"Don't even talk about it," Keith bit off. "Didn't happen."

Elise laughed and entered the elevator when it chimed open. "Better stop betting on them; you're going to lose all your money." She hit the button for the fifth floor.

"You should be more loyal to our team," he said with a smile. "You're a terrible New Yorker."

The doors began to close. "You know I hate baseball, Keith."

He mimicked being stabbed in the heart just as the doors shut.

When the elevator doors opened on the fifth floor, Elise was still laughing to herself. She made it to the third office on the left and unlocked the door with ELISE FANNING - PRIVATE INVESTIGATOR written on the glass in gold lettering. Her office consisted of large bank windows lining the back wall, revealing a beautiful New York City skyline. Her wood-and-brass writing desk sat in front of a red-brick wall, with a filing cabinet on the right. In front of her desk were two client chairs. There wasn't room for anything else, and she didn't need more. It was primarily a place to meet clients.

Once seated, she set her now-empty to-go mug down and removed her laptop from her bag and powered it up. Then she moved to the filing cabinet that wasn't of the normal variety. It was a gift from a friend. The very person she needed to call today. After using the fingerprint scanner, the cabinet opened and she grabbed the burner cell.

"Morning, sunshine," Penny Larson, technology wizard, answered on the first ring. "Please tell me you've got something good for me. I'm bored out of my mind."

"I think I might have something that's going to make your day."

"Oh, tell me."

Elise explained her conversation with Archer last night. Penny already knew about the sex club. She was the one who'd hacked her way past Archer's cybersecurity to get Zoey into Phoenix.

"Well, I'm not surprised Archer outsourced this," Penny eventually said after Elise finished. "You are the best."

"*We* are the best," Elise corrected. "I couldn't do this without you."

"Well, that is true," Penny laughed.

Meeting Penny had been a fluke. Three years ago, after Elise finished her mentorship with the greatest PI in New York City, Luke Hicks, she'd been working on a case for a wife who suspected her husband of cheating. Penny was working for that husband, trying to bury his secrets. Elise found Penny at the end of her investigation, and they'd been working together ever since. Splitting commissions. Kicking ass. "I'm going to courier the mask over to you. Can you take a look at it? And dig a little into the club. See if anything stands out to you."

"You got it."

"Perfect," Elise said, grabbing an envelope. "You'll be in touch when you've got something?"

"You know it."

The phone line went dead. Elise tossed the burner phone back in her cabinet and locked it. After a quick review of her case this morning, she packed up her bag, sent the mask off with the courier, and took the subway to Midtown Manhattan.

Busy streets greeted her as she trotted up the subway's staircase. It took ten minutes for her to arrive at the apartment where her latest client lived. Margaret Wadsworth was an outrageously rich sixty-year-old woman on a full-blown power trip. She hadn't hired Elise because of a broken heart. She wanted evidence against her cheating husband so she could take him to court to get more money. Sad. But the truth was, these cases paid well. Elise could never charge someone who was really suffering of a broken heart her usual rate. So, when a gold-digging woman or rich scumbag came along, she'd up her rates to cover the difference. Most wealthy people didn't blink an eye at her prices. Certainly not Mrs. Wadsworth.

She took a seat on a bench across the street from 15 Central Park West. A place you only lived if you were a multi-millionaire. Trying to remain discreet, she slid on her sunglasses, even though the day was cloudy, and grabbed out the camera phone Penny had given her. The quality of the camera could rival any full-sized one on the market.

It didn't take long for Mr. Calvin Wadsworth to make her job easy. The doorman opened the door, and Mr. Wadsworth came outside with a young brunette who had a slim body and a model's face. Having no shame, he hailed a cab, and before his lover got in, he kissed her like he was going off to war and not planning on coming back.

Elise began snapping pictures. She hated these cases, always had. They only reminded her how hard marriage was and why she didn't do love. Her parents' marriage had been abusive for as long as Elise could remember. She remembered the fighting between her parents that went on for hours, the horrible things her father said to her mother. Love only hurt people, and Elise wanted nothing to do with it. Over the years, she'd had a few long-term friends-with-benefits who worked for a while. Lately, she spent time with one guy who was studying to become a doctor and was too busy to date. Another was an asshole who broke hearts often. But they all had one thing in common. They didn't want love from her. No attachment. Just fun. Eventually, they either moved away or found a woman who wanted more. No skin off Elise's back. Love was meant for other people, not for her.

When her cell phone rang, indicating a FaceTime call, she quickly finished taking photos of the evidence she needed, then hit answer, spotting Zoey's picture on the screen. "Hi, you."

"Hey." Zoey smiled. A natural beauty, Zoey had light hazel eyes that never needed much makeup and gorgeous long strawberry-blonde hair that always looked good no matter what she did with it.

Warmth immediately touched Elise's chest. She missed living with Zoey, who'd moved into Rhys' condo a few days ago. "How's it going?" she asked, angling her phone to keep the sun's glare away.

"Good. Busy, as always," Zoey said. "Listen, I've got to be quick, but I was just talking with Archer."

"Oh, and what did Big Bad Wolf say today?"

Zoey laughed. "Please call him that in front of me. Just once. Okay?" At Elise's responding smile and nod, she went on, "He told me you'd be going to the club tonight to investigate."

News to her. "When did he decide this? He hasn't said a word to me."

"He just left here, so maybe he's planning to call you now. Anyway, I wanted to assure you that neither Rhys nor I will be at the club tonight."

"Thank you for that small miracle. As much as I love you, Zoey, I really don't want to watch you and Rhys getting it on."

Zoey laughed, but she also didn't comment, which had Elise thinking she wouldn't care as much as Elise did. Maybe that made sense. Zoey did like going to Phoenix, living that erotic lifestyle. Elise couldn't imagine having sex in front of others. Ever. "Thanks for thinking of me, though. Appreciate it."

Zoey blew her a kiss. "Always. Love you." Her gaze flicked up to something, then she nodded before addressing Elise again. "Sorry, babe. Got to run. Enjoy tonight."

The last thing Elise needed was anyone getting the wrong idea. "There will be no enjoying. I'm there for a job. Remember?"

"Right," Zoey said with a sly smile. "Then, I hope the job goes well."

"Me too. Talk soon. Bye."

"Bye."

Zoey's endearing, knowing smile was the last image on the screen before it went black. With a sigh, Elise tossed her phone into her bag right as a truck rolled to a stop in front of her. Both a spike of desire and annoyance raced through her as she spotted a smirking Archer looking down at her. It only irked her more that the first thing she noticed was the sexy flex of his forearm and bulging veins. She thought they had a truce between them, but obviously, he was keeping tabs on her, trying to stay one step ahead of her. She wouldn't give him the satisfaction of thinking she cared that he'd likely tracked her cell phone to discover her location. Or that he'd used Zoey to do it. The smart jerk. "Yes, do you need something?" she asked him.

That sexy smile widened. "Just thought I'd confirm you're good to come to Phoenix tonight."

She gave a polite smile, ignoring the heat pooling low in her body that always came when he looked at her like he planned to have her for breakfast, lunch, and dinner. "Yup, all good."

"Great," Archer said. A beep on her cell phone had him adding, "That is the address for a doctor you can go see this afternoon. He'll rush your test results so you'll have them this evening. It's protocol at the club to have a clear STD and HIV test before you can enter."

She frowned. "But I—"

"It doesn't matter if you're not participating," he stated firmly. "Protocol is protocol."

At that, she gave him a small smile. "Is this when you ask me my permission to vet me?"

"I don't need to," he said. "You've already been vetted."

She frowned. Yeah, when his hacker dug through her personal computer.

Before she could get into that, her phone beeped again. Archer said, "That's the address where you need to go. You'll meet up with Lottie, who will dress you."

She snapped out of the swirling heat between them. "Dress me?"

"She'll provide you with a mask and lingerie for this evening, which is appropriate attire for Phoenix." Whatever expression had crossed her face made his eyes darken, filling them with hunger. "I'll see you tonight."

Before she thought about it, she sputtered, "You'll be there?"

His gaze fell to her lips, which she suddenly realized she was biting, and stayed there a moment before he chuckled, low and deep. "Yeah, Elise, I'll be there."

Then he was gone, and she was staring at his tailgate with the feeling she was in way, *way* over her head.

3

---

*T*he look of desire burning in Elise's eyes earlier stayed with Archer for the entire day. So did his semi-erection from the images playing on his mind of her wearing a mask and lingerie for tonight's show. The sound of a piano drifted into Archer's office while he sat behind his desk, wrapping up paperwork for the day. A couple of nights a week, a classical pianist performed at the cigar lounge. The music reached in and touched him, and it sounded like whoever had created the song knew how it felt to yearn. He understood that feeling. Remembered being far away during a mission and missing the comfort of home and the people in his life.

The time on his laptop read 8:55 PM. He'd already briefed his security team on the night ahead, and with his tasks behind him for the day, he left his desk and moved to the bookshelf to the left of the closed door. By removing the third book, he uncovered a keypad and entered in his five-digit code. A soft click later, and Archer opened the book-case, revealing a staircase winding down to the lower level that led to a stone hallway. As he passed the doorway that led to the west tunnel, the door opened. His good friend, Kieran Black, greeted him with a smile. A firefighter with the New York City Fire Department and a triathlete, Kieran could hold his own against any soldier Archer had served with during his time in the military.

"You're almost late," Archer said, returning the smile.

Kieran had strong, trusting green eyes and textured dirty-blond hair, presently slicked back with sweat. "*Almost* is the key word there." Archer and Rhys met Kieran through private sex parties over the years.

Kieran settled into stride with Archer, heading down the hallway, and Archer noted the soot stains on Kieran's cheek. "Busy day?" he asked.

"Yeah," Kieran grumbled. "Insane five-alarm fire down by The Battery. Took us all day to get it under control."

Archer entered the changing room off to the right, remembering what it was like to be in danger for a job. He had a bullet wound as a constant reminder to never take his life for granted. "No injuries?"

Kieran followed him in. "Thankfully, none."

Throughout the space, masks rested on rows of metal shelves above red velvet benches. Some full-face, demonic masks, others more of the masquerade variety. Every time Archer entered Phoenix, he did his best to keep his identity hidden by wearing fuller masks. He preferred to keep his identity from any woman he had sex with, mostly because he was the one who vetted them, and it seemed the professional thing to do. Privately, he didn't want the headache if anyone got attached. While he liked his sex wild and passionate, he never dated anyone he met through Phoenix. But tonight, he wanted Elise to recognize him. To see him with his shirt off. To see all of him. His cock twitched in his pants in full agreement.

When Kieran took off to the shower, Archer quickly went

into the other one. By the time he was dressed in his black slacks and nothing else, the low voice in his Bluetooth earpiece said, "Elise Fanning has arrived. Forms are complete. Test results are negative. She's been dressed, and Lottie has taken her into the main room."

"Thank you," Archer responded to a security teammate and retired Navy SEAL, Hawke Foster, pressing the communicator. He grinned at Kieran, who was watching him closely. "Elise has arrived."

"Ah, so that's what the excitement on your face is all about," Kieran said with a laugh, grabbing a gold mask off the shelf closest to him. "What's up with you and Elise anyway?"

"Tension." Archer reached for the bottle of oil in the glass container left for them. An obvious request from a member tonight.

Kieran rubbed the oil on his chest. "Do you plan on playing with that tension tonight?"

Archer oiled himself up, the shininess detailing every muscle. "Depends."

"On?"

"If she'll let me." He grinned.

Kieran's laugh filled the room as they left the changing room and entered the lounge area. Archer always swore he could nearly taste the lust and seduction on the air in here. Brown leather couches—where women in scandalous lingerie and shirtless men sat—were set around square coffee tables, with large, dim chandeliers over each. The gas fireplace offered little warmth but set the stage for romance and seduction.

Sitting on one of those couches was the fourth in their inner circle of friends, Hunt Walker, who'd come into Archer's life through Kieran. They all came from different walks of life, but the band of brothers were exactly what

Archer needed after leaving the military. More than friends; now chosen family. A New York City Detective, Hunt had light-brown eyes that displayed his strong character, but his messy golden-brown hair softened the sharp edges of his cheekbones. He acknowledged their arrival with a nod, but his attention went firmly back to the star of the show tonight. Lottie, the pretty brunette with the amethyst-colored eyes currently chatting with a couple of members while sipping a glass of champagne. Hunt had eyes for her, only for her. The exact reason he had yet to be put in a show with her. Rhys had a half-dozen men in his roster for the shows his members paid to watch. Most of the women who partook in those shows only did so once. Rhys preferred to keep the experience fresh and exciting. But the participants Rhys kept on were beloved by the members. While Archer, Hunt, and Kieran were among them, so was Lottie.

Archer scanned the room, searching out Elise. It didn't take long to find her. She'd garnered a crowd. One look at her and he knew why. His cock hardened so quickly he bit back a groan. She wore a stunning, strappy red lace teddy. Her hair was straight with a few strands just touching the top of her breasts while the rest lay down her smooth back and stopped at the top of her thong. But the cherry on top was her stilettoes. They made her legs a mile long and damn near the most delectable thing he'd seen in his life.

"Careful, you look like a man who has eyes for no one else."

Archer glanced sideways at Kieran. "Believe me when I tell you she'd kill me before I ever got the chance to fall for her." Whatever he had with Elise wasn't romantic; it was purely sexual. Raw. Dirty. But...*different.* He couldn't quite put his finger on what it was, either.

Kieran's laugh followed Archer as he approached her.

With his smaller mask, everyone in the room knew who he was. It was his job to know who they were and what secrets they held. But the one person he knew the least was also the one he couldn't get out of his damn head.

Elise was laughing at something billionaire Kyle Smart said before she caught Archer approaching. Her laughter died, eyes widened a little, and her heated gaze raked over him from head-to-toe, creating an unquenchable thirst inside him. Not surprising. This kind of chemistry was a two-way street, and Archer knew without a doubt, as much as Elise wanted to strangle him, she also wanted to fuck him. She might want to continue playing games, but he didn't like games; he liked action.

"Good evening," Archer said by way of greeting when he reached Kyle. "Would you mind if I borrow our beautiful guest for a moment?"

Kyle inclined his head. "By all means." He gave Elise a wide grin full of promise. "I hope to see you later."

"Likewise," she smiled, then took Archer's outreached hand.

Her fingers felt just right in his hand, not too strong to show haughtiness, not too light to speak of weakness. *Perfect.* He led her to the far table, away from prying ears. "So," he said when she pulled her hand from his and lifted her wine-glass to her lips. "What are your thoughts so far?"

She swallowed her drink, keeping her attention on the crowd. "That there are a lot of rich people in this room."

He chuckled and took a champagne glass from the server as he walked by, then leaned against the table between them. "What else?"

She scanned the room before looking back at Archer. "I'd say that most people here have one thing in common."

"What is that?" Archer asked, stuck on how beautiful her eyes looked surrounded by all the smoky eye makeup. Even more enticed by the deep-red lipstick covering her pouty lips.

Lips that curved slightly at the corners. "They're passionate."

Archer tipped his glass toward her in agreement before he sipped his champagne, tasting crisp and fruity undertones, and studied the crowd. "Is anyone standing out to you?" he asked, glancing her way again.

"That guy with the black crow's mask." She gestured right. "And that woman in the teal lingerie."

Isaac Shae, the son of an oil tycoon. And Connie Mora, an actress, the very woman Archer wanted investigated, only confirming his instincts were spot on. But that brought up the question—is Isaac involved too? Both were new members, joining a few weeks apart, just over a month ago. Though Archer did all the vetting and Wayne ran a deeper search, nothing about these two had raised suspicions. "Why them?" he asked, keeping his voice neutral so he would not lead her in any direction.

"Because they're not horny."

Archer nearly spit out his champagne. He coughed quietly then whirled to her. "Come again?"

Elise gave a sly smile, her long hair falling over her bare shoulder, sweeping over the side of her breast. "I wouldn't think such a word would rattle you so much, Archer." When he didn't reply, surprised by her unusual lightheartedness, she gestured out. "Look around this room. Every single person is ready to rip each other's clothes off and go at it at full throttle."

Archer tore his gaze off her mouthwatering cleavage and looked around. She wasn't wrong. Even he was ready to rip her clothes off and go at it. He'd grown used to Elise's strong personality and liked it, but this light, playful side matched by the sparkle in her eyes was new and rocked the ground beneath him.

"See how everyone is leaning into each other?" she continued, her voice soft next to him. "Touching each other. Licking lips. Laughing. It's a very sensually charged space, and everyone but those two is acting as they should."

Archer studied them, knowing he never would have noticed that. He needed fresh eyes in this space, and apparently, he needed Elise's eyes.

"So, you've got to ask yourself, why?" Elise continued. "Why are they not responding like everyone else?"

He frowned. "Good question."

She took another long sip of her drink, her gorgeous lips wrapping around the edge of the wineglass. Archer imagined those lips wrapped tightly around him, slowly dragging over his hardened flesh, as she asked, "So, is she the one raising all your inner alarms?"

Rock-hard now, he tore his attention off her mouth and nodded as soft music began to play and the double doors on the far side of the room opened, drawing the crowd forward. "Let's talk more later tonight. I'll give you names, and we can go from there."

"Okay," she said, studying the crowd slowly beginning to enter the room. She turned back to him with a sly smile. "Is this the part when things get interesting?"

Archer polished off his champagne and placed the empty glass on the table before he closed in on her. He took her chin, encouraged by her sharp intake of breath as he let the hunger she stirred in him show. "This is when you decide if you want to leave or stay for the show."

Cheeks burning bright, alongside her heated gaze, her mouth fell open, no sound escaping.

Finally, he'd rendered her speechless...and looking like everyone else in this space: horny. He grinned as pure masculine pride rushed through his veins, then he headed for the doorway. And before she could ask him anything, he turned back to her, placing a new challenge between them he hoped she'd answer. He opened his pants, letting his cock spill free.

EVERYTHING sane and sensible in Elise's mind told her not to walk through those double doors. She hadn't come to watch a sex show. One that Archer was apparently taking part in. She certainly had zero interest in this erotic lifestyle. Sure, she liked her sex spicy—the more passionate, the better—but she didn't like prying eyes getting off on watching her. And yet, one look at his naked form, pure muscle, all hard and *big* man, had her feet moving her in that direction, curiosity driving her steps forward. But as she moved closer, catching his grin and challenging *hot* stare daring her to follow, he turned toward the door, revealing muscles upon muscles, stretching and flexing, as he walked through it, all leading down to the finest sculpted ass she'd ever seen in her life. A glance up revealed a large scar on his shoulder, an obvious gunshot wound from his military career. When he vanished through the doorway, she kept walking until she stepped into the small round room with high stone walls where the crowd stood. Back in the 1920s, she suspected the space was used to store whiskey barrels, the oaky scent still lingering in the dry air.

In the middle of the room, a light-haired man with a gold mask, who she knew for certain was Archer's close friend Kieran, was kissing Lottie, the brunette she'd met earlier. Next to them stood Archer, waiting, but he wasn't looking at them. His smoldering gaze beneath his black masquerade mask was right on...*her*. Her breath hitched under the weight of that stare. Everything lit up inside her at the way he overwhelmed her, awakened her in a way she'd never experienced before, bringing uncontrollable heat into her core. She'd never seen this side of him. He'd never shown her this. The need. The want. The hunger. And she felt the crowd around her drift away as he pulled her in to something new, something foreign, something...*special.*

Even as Lottie broke off her kiss with Kieran, turning her attention onto Archer, sliding her hand into his hair, drawing him forward for a slow opened-mouthed kiss, something shifted in Elise. Primal and desperate, she began to tremble. And with every deep kiss Lottie took from him, it only made Elise want to be that woman, feeling the slow and sensual swipe of his tongue, experiencing his passion. His fire.

Her chest fluttered as Lottie broke away and Archer pinned Elise with his stare again. It occurred to her then that this was his game tonight. His way to tease her, to tempt her, and as her nerve endings stirred and tingled, she realized his plan worked. Her nipples puckered, aching for his sculpted mouth, and her sex clenched, hot and tight, craving his thick hardened length filling her.

Archer kept his gaze locked on Elise as Lottie moved to a small gold tray with a bowl on top. Kieran took a seat on a red velvet chaise with gold accents, and Archer followed, sitting next to him, both looking like Greek gods awaiting their pleasure. Only then did Archer look away. Elise exhaled the breath she hadn't known she was holding and quickly took in the room. There was only one door, with Phoenix members either standing or sitting in the chairs situated around the room. The lust in the space was nearly suffocating, and she soon felt the spiral of erotic freedom surround her when Lottie knelt between the men and dripped oil on Kieran's cock before doing the same to Archer too. They groaned low as Lottie began stroking both men, slowly, sensually.

Elise became lost, not in the way the woman was touching the men, but in the way pleasure washed over Archer's face. The way every muscle flexed. The way his sculpted lips parted, drawing in more air. The need burning in the depths of his eyes behind his mask. Eyes that again stared right at Elise, like a challenge, like a promise.

She knew she should feel embarrassed, shocked...*something*...watching this, but she was absorbed in the moment. In him.

The play continued, the silence broken by the low moans escaping both men and the sucking sounds of Lottie's hands working over them. Until her hands began pumping, hard and fast. Elise's legs trembled under her, her breathing rapid, nearly in tune with Archer's, feeling like that was her hand, her offer of pleasure.

Soon Kieran's head tipped back, his chest heaving. Seconds felt like minutes as his body flexed under the pleasure, and just as he froze, looking mere moments away from erupting, Lottie dropped his cock with a wicked smile. His strangled groan filled the room, and Lottie laughed sensually.

She turned her focus on Archer, holding the base of his cock and pumping hard and fast. Until...he got there too, and right as he nearly came, she let go. Archer growled incoherent words, and Elise felt them brush across her like a sensual touch.

Long minutes passed as Lottie brought the men to the brink of orgasm repeatedly, only to deny them that right.

Tension tightened Elise's core with each denial, her breath caught somewhere deep in her throat. She'd never edged a man herself, but she now understood the draw of such pleasure. Every muscle in Archer's body was strained. Veins bulged in his neck and forearms, and he shook in the best way possible, on the very edge of losing all control. And yet, his gaze was steady and strong on Elise, like she was his anchor. In the sane part of her mind, she never would have imagined watching another woman touch a man would turn her on, but maybe it wasn't about the touching and more about the man. This man. One who created an unexplainable need in her. With an ache that burned deep in her soul, she decided, tonight, she'd give in to the tension building between them for weeks. She didn't know when, but sometime soon, she'd take him to her bed.

"Finish him."

Elise blinked back into focus, locked into Archer's smoldering gaze, realizing someone from the crowd had given the order. She took quick stock and noticed Archer's other good friend Hunt was also in the room, but he seemed only focused on Lottie pleasuring his friends.

A low grunt sent her focus back to Kieran as Lottie stroked him, hard and fast, with the intention of ending this show. Kieran lasted a mere second before his shout echoed in the room as he came with a roar, completely undone. Lottie slowly released him, leaving his semen covering his stomach and sat back on her knees.

"Now the other."

Another order from the crowd, making Elise realize it must have come from the member who'd requested this particular show tonight. But this time, Lottie didn't take Archer's cock and finish him. She rose and moved out of the way, her playful stare meeting Elise's. Elise spotted the tremble in Archer's legs as he rose. Eager and hard, his body a glorious display of strength, he made his way toward her with powerful strides.

A wave of heat rocked her to her core as he stopped in front of her. He began to circle her, trailing his finger slowly down her arm. "Do you think I didn't know?" he asked.

She felt the others watching her, their eyes following her every move, only she couldn't seem to find the part where she cared. "Didn't know what?" She heard the lust vibrating in her own voice.

Once behind her, he leaned in close, his mouth by her ear, his voice husky. "Your little brush-of-your-hand trick to see if I was hard yesterday. I wanted you as much as you wanted me." He slid a finger under her hair, moving it aside to place a light kiss on her shoulder, and she trembled, her breath all but gone.

As he got back in front of her, her chest heaved. "It wasn't a trick. It was a curiosity."

He dipped his chin. His mouth curving slightly. His eyes blazing hot. "Now you know I want to fuck you. What are you going to do about it?"

She shuddered. Totally and completely shuddered for all to see. Archer saw it too. His smile was a little sexier now, darker. "Is that my choice here?" she asked, suddenly feeling those watchful eyes fade away as palpable passion overwhelmed her.

He inclined his head. "I'm right here, burning for you. You want me; take what you want."

It occurred to her then that she'd been a part of the show from the very beginning; she simply hadn't known it. And by the big grin on the face of the man who'd been talking to her earlier, she was there as part of his show. But the challenge in Archer's gaze was there, the dare strong, and while she'd never been this bold, she rejected weakness. Every bit of it. If Archer could do this, she could do this. Their level of security made her feel safe. And for just this night, she decided to give in to the pulsating desire between them.

In the silence, Lottie stepped forward with a sensual grin. "She does not want to finish him, but I do."

Archer stared with a burning challenge, one Elise felt

33

simmering in her own gut. She stepped forward, sliding her hand over the round hard muscle of Archer's bottom, feeling the tremble that rocked him. "No," she said, thrusting her fingers into his hair and pulling his mouth down to hers. "He's mine to finish tonight."

4

*E*lise's kiss shattered him.

Taken aback by the sheer passion she unleashed on him, he froze against its force. He'd kissed many women, but not like this. Never like this. He found her waist and pulled her closer, desperate for not an inch to remain between them. She moaned into him, a sound he'd never known he needed to hear, and everything around him simply went away. There were no eyes watching them. No noise from a crowd. No show he was a part of, only she remained. And this fire she possessed. Fire he wanted to burn him alive.

"Elise," he whispered just for her, nipping at her bottom lip.

She shivered before breaking away, and without a moment's hesitation, she revealed herself to him. She took each thin strap down slowly until the fabric of her teddy brushed across a taut rosy nipple. Her stare was potent, powerful, and he felt the brush of tangible energy across his flesh.

Every single move she made was to tease him, and each movement made his cock twitch. The slight curve of her mouth told him she knew it, too. Hell, she played on it, dragging the fabric down slowly until both her breasts were free. Archer nearly went to his knees before her. The beauty... amazed him. Her long hair flowed around her, her skin creamy and smooth, all in stark contrast to his strength and roughness.

She went to move again, but Archer caught her hand, not allowing her to control all of this. "Let me look at you."

Her chest lifted and fell with heavy breaths as he released her hand to drag his knuckles across her breast, reaching a firm nipple. He trailed those knuckles across the hard peak that begged for his mouth. Taking his time, he opened his hand and caressed the side of her breast until he tickled the underside and her soft moan made him smile. "So responsive." Sliding those same fingers, he worked his way over to her other breast, where he tweaked the bud with his fingers. Her eyes fluttered when he pinched hard, and his smile widened. "Beautiful."

He lowered his hand, feasting upon her toned belly and her cute outie belly button before lifting his attention to her face again. He studied her playful gaze beneath her mask before she slid the lingerie lower and lower until the flimsy fabric hit the floor. It occurred to Archer why people believed in succubi; because if Elise were a demon, he'd give his soul for a single taste of the sweetness hidden behind the dark curls between her thighs.

Determined to do just that, he closed the distance between them as she stepped out of her lingerie. Holding her gaze, he took her chin, brushing his thumb across her bottom lip that parted for him. He dragged his finger all the way down her neck and kept going until he slid two fingers between her thighs, instantly hit with warm silkiness. "So wet. All for me?"

Trembling, looking on the very edge of control, her gaze

flared with challenge as she fisted his cock. "For this." She threaded her hands into his hair, pulling him to her. He chuckled at the power play, then nipped at her neck before she yanked his head up and kissed him again. Hard.

Tonight was her choice, but now she was in his playing field. Determined to take her in the way he'd imagined while stroking himself late in the night, he gathered her in his arms, her thighs wrapping tight around his hips. With every step forward, she rubbed her sex against him, teasing, tempting. Until her back hit the wall a second later and he pinned her arms above her head with one hand, the other pulling her against him, trapping her between him and the wall. He licked down her neck, feeling her shudder before she began grinding herself up and down against him. When he met her mouth, kissing her without restraint, she moved harder, faster. He groaned into her open mouth while their tongues danced.

She wiggled to break free. He growled against her neck, "You won't refuse me what I want."

"You won't refuse me, either." She yanked out of his hold and gave a hard shove. Since he wasn't expecting it, she managed to wiggle away. A devilish smile crossed her face as she pushed on his chest, and he allowed it and backed up, returning to the chaise. She took the condom off the tray and had him sheathed in it a second later.

He grinned at the pride in her eyes. She thought she'd won, and for a moment, he considered letting her, until he caught her spicy scent and he remembered something else he wanted more. When she moved to straddle him, he locked his arms around her waist, flipping her onto her back. She struggled against him, but he pinned her, using his size against her. "Keep fighting." He grinned. "I like it."

Her gaze blazed red-hot. "You're an ass."

"I'm all right with that." He chuckled, then nestled his

head between her thighs, and at the first draw of her musky scent, pre-cum leaked from his cock. She relaxed a little at his first slow taste of her. He licked gently up her lower lips, sucking on them, nipping them whenever she wasn't responsive enough. He teased and tickled until she stopped struggling against him and instead rubbed her sex over his mouth. Only then did he stop pinning her, and he used the flat of his tongue to lick over her clit. She moaned, threading her fingers into his hair, shivering under him, then ground herself against him in a plea he would not refuse.

Using a free hand, he spread open her lips, focusing on her clit, giving her the pleasure she sought. Fast licks followed by hard sucks, and her legs were trembling, quivering with a need to explode. When her moans cut off, her back arching with the force of the pleasure, he sealed his mouth over her and brought her clit gently between his teeth. Then he sucked. Hard.

Elise exploded beneath him, a gorgeous flail of freedom and pleasure.

When her moans turned to whimpers, he gently stroked her with big, long licks, drawing her back from her climax and taking the sweetness of her into him. And with a final soft kiss on her sensitive pinkish flesh, he leaned away, and her eyes fluttered open, a burn in them he'd never seen before.

He'd made her surrender. She knew it, and she didn't like it.

Her knee met his chest, and she sent him back on the chaise. With that feisty look on her face she owned so well, she climbed onto his lap. Back and forth, she rocked herself against him, ruthlessly teasing him as an obvious show of punishment, until she took just the tip of him in and bounced mercifully.

He ground his teeth, locking his gaze with hers, letting her play.

She wiggled atop him, sometimes taking him in a little deeper, but never enough to let him find pleasure or to have what he wanted—all of her. She leaned back, giving him a fine view of her round breasts bouncing with her movements, her long hair tickling his legs when she tilted her head back. But it was the intensity in her gaze when she looked at him again that turned off the reasoning in his mind. The fight she possessed. She brought something primal out in him. Something that declared: claim her.

Done with teasing, he gathered her in his arms, flipping their positions so she lay on her back with her ass hanging off the chaise.

Her lips parted.

"Shut that beautiful mouth of yours," he growled, hooking her legs on his arms. "You're mine to fuck."

Desire consumed him as he felt her relax, and he didn't hesitate. He gripped her arms, pinning her beneath him, and took them both where they needed to go. Over the edge. Together.

Rapid thrusts led to his grunts mirroring her moans. She kept her gaze right on him, like she never wanted to forget this moment. Like she wanted to remember it all, to get off on it later. He drove in harder, faster. Unrelenting. The scent of their sex filling his senses as his muscles strained, his heart racing to rise to the pleasure. There was nothing sweet about this. Nothing that had anything to do with lovemaking. Raw, dirty, and intense, he pounded into her with all his strength.

Until her inner walls squeezed him. He'd been teased too much tonight. Gripping her arms, his balls tightened against the contractions she offered, her screams of pleasure filling his ears. He lost the visual of her as she exploded beneath him, bucking and jerking into her climax. With a soul-deep roar, he followed her.

When consciousness returned to him, he heard her rough breathing by his ear and became aware of his own as he was slumped over her. Sweat coated his skin, as it did hers. Still deep inside her, he blew out a breath, settling the beat of his heart, when sudden clapping had him glancing back over his shoulder. He'd forgotten the crowd was there at all and guessed Elise did too. As a participant in the show, he was meant to put on a long, sensual show to please the crowd, not fuck her wildly. But he had no regrets. Not a single one. He met Hunt's amused gaze behind him—his friend was grinning like a fool—before landing on Kieran, who stood next to a wide-eyed Lottie.

Kieran mouthed *Holy fuck*.

Holy fuck, indeed. And as Archer glanced back to a panting Elise, who had yet to open her eyes, he knew then that what they'd experienced together tonight was as close to heaven as he'd ever get, and he wanted more.

ACHING in all the right places, Elise stepped out of the shower in the changing room. She hadn't realized it at the time, but Archer had oil on his skin, and it had covered every square inch of her by the time they'd both crashed over the edge. She'd never admit this aloud to anyone, but she'd taken a much longer shower than normal to ensure most people had left for the night. What had happened tonight had never happened before, and having sex in front of others was only part of what had her head spinning. She'd never gotten so absorbed in anyone to forget her surroundings completely. It wasn't until Archer helped her into a black silk robe that she remembered a crowd had been there at all. But as she quickly toweled off and redressed in her jeans and thin blouse with a camisole underneath, she started to feel a tightness in her chest at being so exposed tonight. Dear God, she had to face Kieran and Hunt again at some point. She had to face Archer tonight. She should have scoped out the fastest route out of the place.

A thousand unknowns filled her head, becoming all-consuming as the changing room door opened and Lottie entered.

Lottie took one look at Elise's face and said, "Ha! Girl, look at those burning cheeks. It's been so long since I've felt embarrassed; I can't even remember what that feels like."

Elise laughed softly, grabbing her boots and sliding into them. "Tonight was...unexpected."

"Maybe for you," Lottie said, leaning against the wall behind the door, arms folded. "Sure seemed like Archer had a plan tonight."

"Yeah, it did, didn't it?" Elise tried to wrap her head around that, around all of this, but the task seemed impossible.

Lottie gave a short nod. "He's waiting out there for you."

"He is?"

Lottie smiled. "Seems a tad protective of you."

No, they were professionals who were working together. They had a job to do. Lottie just didn't know it. She avoided Lottie's remark and, instead, said, "Thanks for the help tonight, Lottie. Appreciate it."

"No worries. Good to meet you, hon. Hope to see you again." Lottie's eyes sparkled before she turned to the door. "Oh, and, Elise?" She glanced back and added, "I know, for you, this is all new and embarrassing thinking you had sex with others watching, but for us, this is very normal. Being naked, having sex, and watching that sensual bond, it's our way of life. Anyone who watched

41

you tonight would only have been thinking how absolutely beautiful you looked and were grateful to take a peek into your passion. So, zip up the embarrassment, okay? It has no place here."

She left through the door before Elise could respond, leaving her reeling. She didn't know how to feel about this, beyond embarrassed, but as she lifted a boot on the bench and began zipping it up, she realized that's all this was an *experience.* A crazy, wild fantasy she'd never wanted but had fulfilled anyway. So, she listened to Lottie and stuffed her shyness away. Even if her heart kept saying, *yeah, keep telling yourself that.*

Once her face cooled enough to save her from further embarrassment and her strength snapped back into place, she exited the changing room and found Archer leaning against the wall. She saw no heat in his eyes, and oddly, she missed the way his gaze had sizzled for her earlier. She waited for his regular haughtiness to rise, especially since she'd given herself to him, but his face revealed nothing.

"Good to go?" he asked, his emotions locked up very tight.

She nodded. "Definitely."

He gestured down the hallway. "Come on. I'll walk you to the subway, and we can talk about the case."

"Sounds good to me." She followed him through a doorway on the right that led to a staircase and exited through the bookshelf in his office. "Neat trick."

He closed the bookcase. "This entire place is a maze of secret passageways and tunnels."

Everything about Phoenix was full of mystery, which was probably why so many people paid excessive amounts of money to live out their fantasies here. As Elise followed Archer outside and they were heading toward the subway station, she kept waiting for an awkward moment to rise, but it simply never came. Being around Archer had been easy before the sex and, surprisingly, was just as easy after.

"About tonight," he said, shoving his hands into the pockets of his jeans. "Any regrets?"

"None."

He gave her a quick look before setting his gaze back on the sidewalk. "Not feeling anything at all?"

Her stomach roiled at his directness. She didn't do feelings. Not well anyway. "How are you feeling about what happened between us tonight?"

The side of his mouth arched, a telling sign he read right through her avoidance. "Happy. Relieved. And intrigued."

She couldn't go there. Talk about emotions and things. She never went there, not with anyone but Hazel and Zoey. Keeping the focus on him, she asked, "Why intrigued?"

He glanced sideways, grinned a little. "I'm just trying to figure out how you can fuck with enough passion to blow the world apart."

She laughed softly. "It's a talent."

She expected him to laugh back, but he didn't. He set that intense stare on her again, his eyes searching hers like he was looking for something. Sure, she felt the tug to learn more about him, but she couldn't tiptoe past the emotional line. She didn't have a great opinion of relationships. Until everything lined up perfectly with a man, she'd never commit to anyone. And it hadn't lined up yet. To get the subject back to things not involving emotions, she asked, "All right, tell me the names of the two people I pointed out to you tonight."

"Connie Mora. She's an actress. And Isaac Shae, the kid of an oil tycoon."

She'd seen a movie with Connie in it but hadn't heard about Isaac before. "I think it's safe to say she's up to something if both of us get weird vibes from her. Did you get anything from Isaac?"

"No, I didn't," Archer said as they passed beneath a street-light. "Did you get a look at them during the show?"

She cringed. "I might have been too preoccupied to notice their behavior during the show."

His smile was so damn proud. "Couldn't take your eyes off me, huh?"

She rolled her eyes. There was the haughtiness that drove her crazy...and made her armor snap up. "It's kind of hard to look away from two men being nearly tortured by their orgasms."

"Mm-hmm," was all the jerk said, his grin widening.

"Moving on," she said, getting the conversation back to important things. Like the case. "Regardless, their behavior was weird enough earlier in the night that I still get the feeling it's not their scene. So, that begs the question: why are they there?"

They reached the subway station, and Archer stopped at the top of the stairs, turning back to her. "Do you have ways to answer that particular question?"

"Of course I do. It might just take a bit of time to get there."

His eyes searched hers again. "All right. Will you need another night at Phoenix?"

She shook her head. "I don't think so, unless I need to see them again for whatever reason."

A pause. Then all that heat he'd been apparently with-holding rose in the depth of his eyes. "Do you want to come back not for investigatory reasons?"

She fought off a shiver even though the night was warm. "As a member, you mean?"

He inclined his head. "I could speak to Rhys on your behalf."

"Thanks, but no. I meant what I said. I really have no

interest in watching other people get it on." The second the words left her mouth, she realized her mistake.

Of course, he grabbed onto it and smiled. "Ah, but you certainly enjoyed watching me tonight."

Her instincts told her to hurry down the stairs and leave this conversation alone, but she knew better. Archer was a friend, one she'd see all the time because of Zoey. They needed transparency. "Listen, I'm going to say something that's going to puff up your pride, but try to restrain it, will you?"

He laughed out loud, easily, in a way she'd never heard from him before. "I'll try. Go on."

She was sure she was later going to regret what came out of her mouth. "Tonight, I wasn't looking at anyone else in that room. I wasn't looking at Lottie with Kieran. I wasn't looking at Lottie touching you. I wasn't feeling the crowd watching me and getting off on that. I was looking at you."

He went still. "So, the fantasy of the club itself did nothing for you?"

"No."

A slow-building smile crossed his face. "*I* was all you wanted?"

Damn, she'd given him far too much. Determined to get back on top of the power...*again*, she closed the distance. As he dipped his chin, she grabbed the front of his shirt and tugged him closer. "What exactly do you want here, Archer? Do you want me to tell you that seeing you tonight drove me crazy? That if I close my eyes, all I can see is how fucking sexy you looked? That I want you again, and again, and again?"

Dark eyes held hers, and he gestured her forward with a flick of his chin. "Have at it, then."

She licked her lips, purposely drawing all his attention to her mouth. She pressed herself against the heat and hardness of his body. "Is that what you want? Do you want me to kiss you again? Fuck you again?"

"It's a good place to start," he murmured.

She brushed her nose against his, feeling the need welling up in her core. But to give him this would be to give the game to him. Tonight, he'd won in a spectacular way, but she was already too unsteady on her feet. "Better not complicate things." And she quickly stepped back.

He grunted. "You are evil."

She laughed, fully aware of the cold void at the absence of his body. "Sometimes, but we've got a job to do. That comes first." Feeling much steadier and liking the arousal burning in his expression, she headed for the subway stairs.

"Elise." She froze on the fourth step and glanced back at him to catch his smile. "I'm really starting to enjoy this *job*."

She smiled and then finished trotting down the stairs. So was she.

5

"*I* heard you and Elise put on quite the show last night," Rhys said the following morning when Archer entered his office with two to-go coffee cups in hand.

Archer noted the laughter behind Rhys' hard gray eyes as he sat behind his huge cherrywood desk in the center of his office, surrounded by bookcases and art. Six foot two, with styled jet-black hair, Rhys came from old money, and he always had an air of authority. Much like Archer had seen in top military officials. But he never wore that wealth in a negative way.

"Heard about that, did ya?" Archer grinned, handing Rhys a paper coffee cup.

Rhys removed the lid of his drink. "When two people practically shake the walls in my club with their lust, yeah, I hear about it."

Archer remembered every moan, every gasp, every touch Elise gave him. He remembered the passion, the sheer explosion when his hands had caressed her. He couldn't stop thinking about her perfect mouth and the unforgettable way she'd kissed him. He also remembered her choice to not come back to the club. He thought that would bother him. The club, the eroticism, it had driven his life. But only Elise was on his mind when he woke this morning, and she'd remained there ever since. He had no intention of over-looking that. "She's quite the woman," Archer said honestly. "A pain in my ass, most definitely, but I can't say I've ever met anyone like her."

"She's a good woman," Rhys agreed, leaning back in his chair. "I'm pleased Kyle's fantasy worked out."

Archer nodded. Kyle's fantasy had been a long-time coming. Yes, he had requested a male-female-male edging fantasy and asked for Archer, Kieran, and Lottie to all partic-ipate. But another one of his requests, one he'd asked for a year ago, but they hadn't fulfilled until last night, was to ask a brand-new member to do the show right in the heat of the moment. That innocence, excitement, nervousness were what Kyle enjoyed. The thought hadn't even occurred to Archer until he saw Elise intently watching him. Then he figured he'd kill two birds with one stone. Get what he wanted, which was to feel that rare chemistry he had with Elise, while also fulfilling Kyle's long-time request. While Elise was in full control of the fantasy and could have walked away had she chosen, Archer was all too glad his instincts were spot on that she'd jump at the chance to finally indulge themselves. "It was definitely for my benefit that Kyle's fantasy worked out."

Rhys smirked. "I suppose it is. Is there something devel-oping there between you two?"

"I'm...not quite sure." Either she simply liked tormenting him with all her teasing last night at the subway and had no plans on letting him have her again. Or, and what he hoped was the case, she was open to seeing where this went.

A pause.

"What?" Archer asked, knowing from a long friendship with Rhys that a pause meant trouble.

Rhys cocked his head and gave a measured look. "Even if things continue casually between you two, I have a few concerns. Two, actually."

"The first?"

"Zoey."

Zoey and Rhys were set to get married sometime next year. Archer took a sip of his piping hot coffee before asking, "How does Zoey come into play here?"

"She's protective," Rhys explained gently. "As protective as we are about each other, I imagine. As my friend, I'd request you tread lightly where it comes to Elise."

Archer snorted. "I don't think I could tread lightly around her if I tried. She runs circles around me."

Rhys' expression became serious, a telling sign he knew something Archer did not. "I suspect she's not all armor. Be considerate of that, is all I'm asking."

All right, so there was more to Elise than Archer knew. Something more to her story that Wayne hadn't felt was necessary to tell him when he dug into Elise's life. Perhaps her strength was a shield to protect a soft heart. Archer doubted she'd ever let him close enough to find out. "All right. I'll keep that in mind."

Rhys inclined his head. "Thank you. Now, my second concern. This morning, I received a call from Rossi. He's requested Elise for his show."

Christopher Rossi was an Academy Award winning actor and a member of Phoenix for a handful of years now. "Never going to happen," Archer stated.

Rhys lifted an eyebrow. "Because you won't allow it?"

"Please." Archer snorted. "We both know that choice does not belong to me and lies with Elise alone."

Rhys offered a sly smile back. "Yes, it is Elise's choice, but it is also my decision whether or not I ask her if she'd like to take part in a show."

Archer should say he had no problem with it. He and Elise weren't together, but... "When is Rossi's show?"

"A couple months away."

Archer blew out a long breath. The stars of the shows always received a gift for participating. Rhys always said it was a way to give back. Rich people paid him for privacy, and Rhys gifted those fulfilling those fantasies money to help them get a better life. "She was pretty adamant last night that she'd never come back to the club, but give her a little time to fully absorb last night's show," he finally decided. "Then I'd be more than willing to do another show with her."

"All right." Rhys slowly grinned, telling Archer he saw right through him.

Even Archer knew his reactions this morning were...*off.* He didn't understand what it was about her that drew him in so forcefully. Last night, he thought they'd kill the tension, the need. This morning, it pulsated worse than ever. He could still smell her, hear her, feel her. His cock throbbed, and before he could harden further, his cell phone beeped in his pocket. He read the screen and wished they were still talking about Elise. "For fuck's sake," he growled.

"What is it?"

"This cannot be a coincidence." Archer studied his phone, reading the article Hawke, one of his team members, sent him. StarCraze was the biggest tabloid gossip column in North America, and the headline read: A SECRET SEX CLUB IN NEW YORK CITY FOR THE RICH AND FAMOUS? WE'VE GOT ALL THE SCOOP! While that was a problem, a big fucking problem, the photograph showed three people. Connie, staring at herself in the gilded mirror in the far corner of the club, Isaac standing behind her, and Kieran off to her right, wearing a gold mask. An outsider wouldn't be able to recognize any of their identities with their faces covered, but Archer knew. "What the fuck is happening here?" He handed his phone to Rhys.

Rhys took one look at the screen, and rage stormed across his expression. "How did this happen?"

"It's Connie—her mask must have had a camera, but how did we not find it?" Archer rose, taking his phone back and texting Kieran. HEADS UP. CHECK OUT STARCRAZE'S ARTICLE. I'M LOOKING INTO IT. BE IN TOUCH SOON. He tossed his cell on the chair he'd been sitting in and thrust his fingers into his hair. "It's got to be Connie and Isaac."

"Isaac Shae?" Rhys snapped.

Archer nodded. "Last night, when Elise came to the club, she said they stood out to her as people of interest."

"Did you tell her we were already looking into Connie?"

Archer paced in front of Rhys' desk. "No. I told her I needed someone looked into, but she wanted to get a feel of the members for herself. Those two stood out to her."

"Why?"

"Because they weren't horny." When Rhys' brows rose, Archer added, "Elise's words, not mine."

"So, their behavior was off?"

Archer nodded. "It's why bringing her in on this was so important. Not only does she have access to places she shouldn't, she's got a real instinct where it comes to investigating people." Archer had seen this in the military. Some people saw the world in a different way, and Elise was one of those people.

Rhys ran a hand across the back of his neck. "We need to get on top of this and find out what they want, especially if they're planning on blackmailing us." He hesitated, then shook his head slowly. "Why the fuck would they publish a photo of themselves when they've paid a hundred grand to keep their identities a secret?"

"I have no idea," Archer replied. "The only logical thing here would be if someone was blackmailing them and their behavior was off because of that?"

Rhys agreed with a nod. "That might be it."

"But why try and sneak a mask into the club if it didn't have a camera? If not on the mask, how the hell did she get a camera in?" Archer countered.

"The amount of unknowns is a big problem." Rhys ran a hand across his face, a heaviness weighing on him. "We're going to have a fallout. Members will leave."

Archer felt each and every one of those words like a punch to his chest. "We'll get this put to bed quickly."

Rhys nodded. "I have no doubt you will." Another pause. "Let's close the club for the time being. I don't want more unnecessary heat, and we want to reassure the members we're taking this breach seriously."

"I'll have the team reach out to everyone today."

"Good." He reached for his coffee again, but then his cell phone rang on his desk. "Harrington," he answered briskly. Immediately, his expression softened. "Sorry, love, it's been a frustrating morning." A pause. "Yes, I'm fine. Is everything okay?" Tension wafted off him when his eyes met Archer's, and then he frowned. "Did this happen last night?" Another long pause. "All right, let me get Archer to find out what's going on. I love you, too. Goodbye." He ended the call and said to Archer, "Elise's office was broken into last night."

"Is this an unusual thing to happen in her line of work?"

Rhys shook his head. "By how upset Zoey is, I'd say it's unusual. She's worried." Archer rose and headed for the door. "Archer." When he looked back, Rhys added, "Elise is very important to Zoey, and Zoey is very important to me. If this break-in is due to her investigating the club, she's off this case and you'll use your friend in Washington."

The friend was a fellow Green Beret, who'd served alongside Archer. He nodded at the order, already a step ahead of Rhys. If whoever did this was tied to Phoenix, he wouldn't continue to put Elise in harm's way.

~

FEW THINGS PISSED ELISE OFF, but as she'd shown Archer with the magazine subscriptions, having her life invaded was one of those things. Papers were thrown about her office and her chair was knocked over. They hadn't been able to crack the filing cabinet. Thank you, Penny.

"Are you okay?"

Heat flooded Elise before she managed to look toward the door. Sure, half naked with a mask, Archer was glorious. But wearing jeans and a gray T-shirt, he was to die for. She could still feel him between her thighs all day. Feel his spectacular kisses and the way they stole the thoughts from her mind. His woodsy scent was a smell she thought she'd never get out of her nose. But it was that smooth, low voice that brought her right back to the best sex of her life. Unimaginable sex. Mind-blowing sex. Sex she wanted again. And again. And again. And then maybe she'd even want it some more. "Yes, I'm okay," she said, glad her voice stayed steady as she reached for some of the papers on the floor. "Is it a fluke you're here, or did someone call you?"

"Zoey called Rhys," Archer said, stepping into her office. "She was worried about you."

Yeah, Elise was worried too. No one had ever broken into her office before. She began gathering up the papers. "I told Zoey not to worry."

"Yeah, well, good friends worry," he countered. "Not much you can do about that." He dropped to one knee next to her, helping with the papers. "You weren't here when this happened?"

"Thankfully, no," she said, unable to meet his gaze, worried about what he'd see in hers if she did. "It must have happened last night."

"You checked security cameras?"

She nodded, goose bumps racing across her arms at his nearness. God, all that heat and strength was so close to her. Too close. "It was the first thing I did when I saw this." She forced herself to look at him, then immediately wished she hadn't. Those penetrating eyes sucked her right in. "One guy broke in. Couldn't make out his face, wore a black hoody."

Archer's gaze fell to the door handle, which was still intact. "How'd he get in?"

"Good ole picking the lock, I suspect." She gave him a hard look. "Speaking of that, how did you get past Keith at the security desk?"

"Charm." He smiled.

She snorted, shaking her head at him, and yet, some of the tightness in her chest began to fade away. "Keith obviously needs a reminder that cute men don't get a free pass into the building."

"Ah, don't be too hard on him. I told him I was here to help you with the break-in and that we were friends."

Friends sounded a whole lot different, rolling off his tongue today. Even she sensed some instability in her. Last night, she'd scratched an itch, expecting that itch to stay gone. But the desire hadn't faded. If anything, it had grown.

Turning away, he helped her gather up the rest of the papers on the floor before he rose again. This time, his expression softened. "I'm sorry for this, Elise."

She moved around her desk to reorganize everything. "Why are you apologizing? You don't even know if it's your case that caused this to happen."

He gave a knowing look. "Do you have any other cases where someone would break into your office?"

"Not at the moment, but this could have been from an old one." Her office was her second home, and the thought of someone touching things made her skin crawl. She picked up files on the floor beside her desk. Files that hadn't been locked away in her cabinet, because they didn't hold secrets.

When she reached for another file, Archer got there first, his hand brushing against hers. Her gaze met his before she could stop herself, and the desire in his stole the air from her lungs. She knew what that desire could do, and she felt the same hunger storm through her.

"We're going to get to the bottom of this," he said, holding her stare and taking her hand.

"We're?" she repeated, hearing the breathiness in her voice.

"Yes, Elise. *We.* Non-negotiable."

She blinked away from the way he captivated her so easily, and yet her breath was uneven. Zoey and Hazel always had her back, but this...*this* was new, and she felt a crack break through her armor. "Well, thank you for showing up to see if I was okay."

"I'm likely the one who put you in this position," he said. "No thank you required."

She slowly pulled her hand away, even though it felt totally wrong to do that. "You didn't put me in any position. Besides, I barely looked into Connie and Isaac last night, except to Google them. What would they even want to find here?"

"None of this makes sense," he said. "Did you see the article this morning?"

"I didn't, but Zoey called. Is Rhys furious?"

"Yes, as he should be. We need to get to the bottom of this."

"We will."

He gave a firm nod. "Let's get you back in order first."

Knowing there wasn't much she could do now beyond that, she turned her focus to her messy office, but she couldn't shake the warmth touching her at Archer's help. Men came and went, never really caring much, but maybe she'd misjudged Archer's haughtiness. Maybe his confidence came from being a good man, and he knew it.

With his help, they finished cleaning up the files, and in no time, she had her office put back together.

"You said you looked into Connie and Isaac last night?" Archer asked, setting the last file into the holder on her desk.

"Yeah, a little."

"Did you do any digging that would warrant this?"

"No," she said, but then she looked out at her office. "But if this is connected to Phoenix, I'd say I hit something someone didn't want me to find."

He nodded, taking a seat in her client chair. "Makes sense. What did you find out?"

"It's all preliminary stuff, really," she explained, sitting in her swivel chair, behind her desk. "Nothing anyone couldn't find on the internet. Just who they are, what businesses they are tied to, income, that kind of stuff."

"So, nothing that jumped out at you as a problem?"

She shook her head. "But…"

"What?"

She didn't want to get ahead of herself, but her instincts weren't usually wrong. "There is a connection between the two; did you know that?"

He cocked his head. "What kind of connection?"

"They used to date."

Archer nodded. "Yes, I was aware, but when we vetted them, it was a nonissue. Connie is married to Isaac's older brother, Elijah. Both had no problem attending the club if the other was there."

At that, Elise froze. "Is Elijah a member too?"

"No," Archer said. "But Connie indicated her husband did not mind her involvement with the club."

"You didn't think to look into that further?"

He frowned. "I'm not people's babysitter. Connie said her husband enjoyed her when she came home from the club. Beyond that, she had no skeletons in her closet that would compromise Rhys or Phoenix. That's all that mattered to me."

"Well, just saying. Apparently, she does have some skeletons you don't know about."

"Apparently," he grumbled in agreement. He sank deeper in the client chair, filling it out completely and stretching out his strong legs. "What are your thoughts on the photograph that was published?"

"First thought: I hope Kieran doesn't have a secret wife who doesn't know he belongs to a sex club."

Archer laughed, the warm sound carried to her core. Trouble, that's what Archer Westbrook was. Pure, hot-as-hell trouble, who seemed to have turned her brain onto permanent turned-on mode. "I can assure you there is no secret wife," he said. "Kieran's on alert and will handle whatever comes his way."

"Good," she said with a nod. "My next thought is just total confusion. Logically, I'm thinking Connie brought in her own mask to take photographs. Maybe she's using tech that either you couldn't see, or she got rid of the camera when she realized she was found out."

"I agree with you," Archer said.

"But—" Elise pondered. "Why would anyone publish a picture of themselves in a tabloid? What could they possibly get from that?" She hesitated, then voiced her thoughts. "Has Rhys made enemies? Could this be to blackmail him?"

Archer shook his head slowly, frustration in every hard line of his face. "I don't have answers to those questions."

"Well, things typically don't make sense until they do."

The side of his mouth curved. "Are those Elise Fanning's words of wisdom?"

"Damn straight, they are."

He laughed again, then rose. "What's your plan for today?"

"I need to look through some security footage to see if I can figure out who broke in here. Then I'll dig deeper into Connie and Isaac."

"All right. I need to go put out some fires with the members. Three of them have given up their membership, and I suspect more will follow." He ran a hand across the back of his neck. "Take the day, and I'll meet you at your place later, and we can continue forging ahead on our case."

"My place?"

He nodded. "Right now, as far as I'm concerned, you're not safe. I put you in this situation. The least I can do is offer you some protection while you work." He paused, and she gawked, so he added with a grin, "I'll sleep on the couch or the floor. I don't need any special accommodation."

Everything inside her head screamed *bad idea*, especially when she was already feeling unsteady on her feet where it came to him. And she was *always* steady on her feet. "Thank you, really, but that's not necessary."

"Elise."

"Archer."

He frowned.

She frowned back. "Honestly, I'm okay. I'll look into who broke in and will call once I've got a name, and if I'm unable to figure out who it was, I'll call the police to report the break-in, so you truly don't have to worry." She gave him her best easy smile, hoping to put his concerns to rest. "I'll even let you go have a chat with them, if you'd like."

He watched her closely, then gave a firm nod. "Keep me updated."

As he headed for the door, she called, "Thanks again for checking in on me."

His eyes softened. "Like I said, you're not in this alone. You need me, just call."

Once he left, she flopped down into her chair, exhaling a long breath and realizing having Archer watching her back wasn't so bad after all.

6

*L*ater that night, after Archer made the hour drive from Manhattan to Brooklyn, he arrived at Elise's loft in a mood. She hadn't called him to update him on who broke into her office. Judging by what he knew of Elise, he figured she had a hard time depending on others, especially those she didn't trust. Oddly, it grated on his last nerve that she didn't trust him. He needed to fix that. But it wasn't only Elise on his mind; five members had walked away from Phoenix because of the breach, and Rhys was not happy. And while it was Archer's team who'd let the camera into the club, the responsibility landed on his shoulders, absolutely destroying any happiness he felt from last night with Elise. He spent the day taking half of the calls Rhys had to make to the members, and luckily, Archer's reassurance that the matter was being handled swiftly calmed the remainder of them down.

With a heavy sigh, he exited the truck, trotted up three floors to Elise's loft, and knocked on the front door.

Footsteps came from the other side until the door opened, revealing Hazel. "Oh, hi, Archer."

"Hey," he said. "Is Elise here?"

"She's actually out for a jog but should be home soon. Is she expecting you?"

He laughed softly. "I'd say no, but I imagine she's probably, as always, one step ahead of me and knows I'd show up here."

Hazel laughed softly and then nibbled her lip. "She might have mentioned you wanted to stay the night to keep an eye on us."

Archer didn't know Hazel too well, but he liked her from what he did know. She had a sweet softness about her and seemed as loyal as Elise. "I'm concerned about the break-in at her office today. I feel like I've put her in a dangerous position because she's working a case for me. I promise to stay out of your way, but until we've got a handle on this, it'll make me feel a whole lot better knowing you two are safe."

Hazel examined him, obviously reading his intentions, then she nodded. "Elise will probably kill me, but okay." She opened the door wider. "I was actually just heading out, but feel free to watch some TV until she gets back."

"Thanks." Archer stepped into the loft just as Hazel headed out. "I'll see you later."

Hazel's mouth twitched. "Yeah, maybe you will."

She headed down the stairwell, and Archer shut the door behind her. Yeah, the *maybe* was because Hazel doubted Elise would go for him sleeping over. He got that, knew Elise was a fighter and liked handling her own business. Hell, he respected that. But he simply had to get her to see why he needed to watch over them. He protected people. He didn't put them at risk. Not in the military. And not now. He also didn't mind getting to know her a little more, finding out what made this woman tick.

In the doorway, he knew as he untied his boots that he was crossing a line, but he also knew Elise. She'd already refused his help, but that was her pride talking. He'd seen the slight shake of her hand when she cleaned up her office. The unsteadiness in her gaze. She was rattled. Until he knew with total certainty she was safe, he'd stay close.

After he kicked off his boots, he took in the space. Her loft was a lot like her. Unique. Stylish. He took a seat on the couch, grabbed the remote control, and turned on the television to watch the sports recap.

Twenty minutes later, the front door opened. "Hazel Rose, you know not to leave this door open—" Elise caught Archer sitting on the couch, and the reprimand fell away. It took every ounce of his strength not to leap up off the couch and erase the distance between them. She was flushed from her run, her hair pulled up in a ponytail. She wore a black sports bra and purple leggings, and Archer wanted to explore every inch of her. Something the rising heat in her eyes suggested she wouldn't mind.

Smart and aware as always, she tilted her head, obviously listening for Hazel. When only the voice of the sports reporter filled the air, she frowned. "You know it's rude to break into someone's house, right?"

He snorted. "I didn't break in. Hazel let me in before she left."

Traitor showed on Elise's expression. "Did she?"

He nodded, enjoying her fierce look, especially since that fierceness was directed his way. "You never called, so I take it you didn't find out who broke into your place?"

"Not yet," she grumbled, shutting the door behind her and locking it. "But I reported the break-in to the police. They sent someone over to fingerprint my desk and door, and I gave them the security tape of the guy, so it's out of my control. We wait for them to get a hit."

"Good, going by the rule book in this case only keeps you safer."

"Mm-hmm," she agreed.

He kept his focus narrowed on her, enjoying watching her shift her hips. He wondered how hot she was between her thighs. "Get any additional details about Connie and Isaac?"

"That might come later tonight," she said. Since she didn't elaborate, he figured she would update him later and kept quiet as she said, "You?"

"They called Rhys separately, both furious that their photographs were exposed in the media."

Her brows furrowed. "Behavior that actually lines up?"

"Yeah," he agreed with a nod. "But something still feels off with Connie. She's just not quite ringing true."

"Then we'll stick with her," Elise said. "How bad was the fallout from the photograph?"

"Bad," he said. "But that's expected. Phoenix members pay for tight security. I failed them." *Let me touch you tonight, and I won't fail you.*

"You didn't fail them. Shit like this happens sometimes." She studied him for a moment, obviously reading his hunger, and her legs parted slightly. "I take it there is nothing I can say that's going to reassure you I'm fine and don't need you to sleep over?"

"Nope." He smiled. "It's the soldier in me, Elise. I'll sleep in my truck if that suits you better, but I'm not leaving until we've got the break-in figured out."

Her skin flushed further before she kicked off her runners. "Okay," she finally said. "Well, if you plan on staying, then wait here. I need a shower before I've got to meet someone later. You might as well come."

Images of her naked and deliciously wet flooded his mind. "Does this someone have something to do with the break-in and our case?"

Her breath hitched, and she shrugged. "Maybe. I mean,

I'm not even sure yet that the break-in has anything to do with our case. But now that I've done all the preliminary work, things can start moving ahead." She gave him a slow-building smile, dripping with lust. "We'll grab some grub on the way. I won't be long."

"Sounds good." When she headed for the door off to the left, his attention drifted to her spectacular ass in her tight leggings. He remembered how she'd moaned a little louder when he'd slapped that ass last night. His cock, growing harder by the second, remembered too. Yeah, he was done with not acting on this heat between them. "Would you like some company?" he called, throwing the offer out there.

She stopped again and glanced over her shoulder with hooded lids. "In the shower?"

"Mm-hmm," he murmured.

Not one to back down from anything, she turned to face him. "Listen, I don't want things to get messy between us. I don't do serious relationships."

He considered that, curious what her hang-ups about relationships were. "I'm not looking for anything serious right now," he told her. Not that he didn't want that, he did, eventually. Back in the military, he'd avoided serious relationships due to the nature of his work and not being home enough to support a healthy relationship, but his life was different now.

"Perfect," she said, biting her lower lip. "We understand each other, then."

He understood that he was done playing with her. He wanted them both to win, every damn time. "Actually, no, I don't think we understand each other at all." He rose and erased the distance between them, enjoying how she watched his every move like she couldn't get enough of him. "Just because we don't want something serious, doesn't mean we can't have something fun." When he purposely got into her space, tasting that rich lust in the air between them, he added, "Do you not want more of what we had last night?"

She slowly began to smile. "Is that what you want? More of last night?"

Tired of her answering his questions with questions of her own, he pressed her. "Don't you?"

Her gaze fell to his lips, then returned to his eyes. This time, her smile was dripping with lust. "I really should get to that shower."

A night of debauchery filled his thoughts as she headed for the bathroom. Those same thoughts intensified as she left the bathroom door wide open, an obvious invitation. The water turned on, and he didn't need to hear more. With powerful strides, he entered the bathroom and shut the door behind him, then turned to her in the shower. She stood beneath the water, head tipped back, soaking herself. Her long hair was free, her back arched slightly, lifting her breasts, while the water ran over the hard peaks of her nipples down to her belly button, all inviting Archer to lick that same path.

He didn't need to see more. He stripped. Hard and ready, he entered the shower with her.

Her eyes snapped open when he got close, and she shook her head with a sensual smile. "Stay there. You like to watch, right?"

"I like watching you," he murmured.

"Then follow the rules," she purred. "Watch, don't touch."

She'd thrown Phoenix's tagline at him, and he smiled at her, letting her take control now. Keeping her gaze locked on him, she ran her hand over her breast and slid her fingers all the way down to between her thighs. She stroked there in lazy movements as her other hand worked its way over to her chest. Her soft moan filled the bathroom, and Archer swallowed deeply as she squeezed her breast and began to circle her hips, unsure for the first time in his life if he could watch and not claim.

He'd seen many beautiful things in his life, but nothing like this. Nothing this perfect. Nothing this real. It occurred to him then that, that's what he liked about Elise. She wore no mask; who she was, was who you got. Overwhelmed by need he could not ignore, he fisted his cock out of pure desperation and began stroking himself to the rhythm she set.

His gaze took its fill. The water rushing over her shoulder, down to her taut nipple that she pinched and played with. When her eyes reopened and she caught Archer following her lazy strokes with pumps of his hand, her speed shifted. Mouth falling open, her hand moved faster now, her gaze staying on him, as her half-lidded eyes filled with uncontrolled passion. *Need.*

Faster and faster, she worked her fingers in circles, pressing deep on her clit. Her breathing became rough, loud, and Archer was right there with her. He pumped his hand, gritting his teeth against the surge of pleasure washing over him.

Until he dropped his cock, not to spill his seed, as Elise broke apart, shuddering, her head tipping back as she moaned, grinding her hips into her hand. He hung on the edge with her, every second longer than the last as this was a punishment far worse than being edged in front of a crowd.

Only when she met his eyes again, sweet satisfaction simmering across her expression, did he continue stroking himself.

Ready to blow, he gestured her forward with a flick of his chin. "Get over here."

A salacious smile filled her face as she took one step, then another. Water dripped from her hair, droplets running down along her breasts. Her breath rushed out when she stopped right in front of him. "Yes, Archer?"

He'd let her play. Even let her control him, to show her he wanted more of her and that he didn't always need to win, but he had his limits. "Look at me." He squeezed his hand around his cock, the water raining down on him. "Don't take your fucking beautiful eyes off me." He groaned into the pleasure, stroking himself, slow, tight.

Her chest heaved with her heavy breathing as he thrust his hand in her hair, staring right at her, and he didn't pause. He stroked himself, none-too gently, swiftly bringing himself to orgasm. Locked onto her, he growled his release. His semen sputtered from his cock onto her stomach, and by the unadulterated passion on her face, she relished him marking her.

*a*n hour later, and full from a burrito they'd grabbed from a street vendor on the twenty-minute drive over to the Bay Ridge area, Elise's body still hummed in pleasure. She looked at this thing with Archer from every angle. Having him—a retired Green Beret—sleep at the house tonight meant Hazel would stay safe in case this break-in turned into something far more dangerous. And while Elise sensed the draw to him was more than anything she'd felt before, when he looked at her like she was the only thing he wanted, there was no turning back. No game she wouldn't play. Even now, sitting in the passenger side of his truck while he drove, one hand slung over the steering wheel, she sensed the building tension, the uncontrollable heat, to have him again.

The thought stayed with her as they approached the long, thin driveway that led back to an old red-bricked warehouse covered in graffiti. "Turn right here," she instructed. "Park by that delivery door there."

In minutes, she was directing him past the delivery door to the small wooden staircase that led to a steel door that needed a new paint job. She glanced up, waved, and smiled at the camera.

The door clicked open.

She had to give it to Archer; he had yet to ask a single question about why they were there, but as she led him through the dimly lit factory with old machinery scattered around, she could see his training kick in. Archer's eyes scanned the area like he knew exactly where the exits were. He didn't glance around a room. He surveyed it, looking for threats and for ways he could hold an advantage.

When they reached the big metal double doors, they slid open, and Elise entered the room where a blonde woman with a messy bun sat behind her big monitors atop her curved desk in the center of the room, classic rock playing through the speaker hanging on a metal pole. Elise noted the way Archer's eyes narrowed as he studied her. "Archer Westbrook, this is Penny Larson. She's my go-to tech wizard."

Archer offered his hand. "Pleasure to meet you, Penny."

Penny was a twenty-five-year-old who'd spent her youth playing video games and learning code instead of going to parties. She wore her typical attire of a T-shirt and jeans. Today her shirt read IT'S TOO PEOPLEY OUTSIDE. She returned Archer's handshake and gave her cute smile that Elise had seen her use many times. Obviously, she thought Archer was hot. And well, he was *hot.* "So, this is the guy with the sex club, huh?" Penny asked Elise.

Archer glanced sideways with a frown, and Elise chuckled. Yeah, she'd purposely left this part out but figured he might not say yes to involving Penny in their business. *It's easier to ask forgiveness than it is to get permission*, as the saying goes. "You can trust Penny. She does a lot of work for me."

Archer's frown deepened, and he shoved his hands into his pockets. Elise sent him a quick smile, but he didn't smile back, clearly putting two and two together that Penny was

Elise's hacker. The same hacker Elise had used to hack Phoenix's system to get Zoey inside.

"Oh, geez, you're so intense," Penny said with a soft laugh. "You can really trust me. Much more than you can trust that dipshit you use for intel."

Archer lifted a single eyebrow. "That dipshit I use for intel?"

"I did tell you, your hacker was dirty," Elise said, then moved to sit on the edge of Penny's desk. It's why she got her revenge with the magazine subscriptions. His dirty hacker went through her personal files. And it was why, after that hack, Elise had asked Penny if she wanted to meet Archer to do some possible work for Phoenix, and Penny had agreed. She'd been waiting for the right moment to gently introduce them. It just so happened that Archer showing up before her meeting with Penny had given her the perfect time to put her plan in motion.

Archer gave them both an incredulous look. "Aren't all hackers a little dirty?"

Penny gasped, a hand on her chest. "Take that back right now!" she exclaimed, pointing to the door. "Or get your sexy ass outta here."

Elise chuckled. She'd never seen Penny so insulted.

Both of Archer's brows rose now, his mouth twitching. "I apologize and take it back. Why is Wayne dirty?"

The tightness in Penny's eyes lessened. "Some of us do good work. We only hack to help people, not to hurt. I am one of those people."

"And Wayne isn't?"

Penny shrugged. "I mean, he's not the worst, but I know for a fact he's done a few things that wouldn't get him on Santa's nice list."

"Then I suppose I should fire him," Archer said.

Penny smiled again, her voice bubbly, "Yes, you should."

She spun in her chair, looking back at her monitors and clicking away on her keyboard. "I work for good people. Like my girl here." She gestured to Elise. "Only the ones out there fighting the good fight."

Elise felt the heat of Archer's stare, but instead of getting caught up in it, she pushed ahead, "Today, my office was broken into," she told Penny.

Penny turned to face her. "Shut up!"

"Yeah, I wasn't happy either," she grumbled. "I couldn't find anything on the building's surveillance except for a guy who picked my lock. Couldn't see his face."

"Did he take anything?"

Elise shook her head. "Nothing that I could see, but he also couldn't get into my locked files."

"Of course he couldn't." Penny grinned from ear to ear, always proud of her work. "Okay, I'll see what I can find."

"Thanks. I called the police to get it on record, and they came out to fingerprint the door and stuff. Might want to keep an eye on their files to see if they get a name." Sure, she trusted law enforcement to do their jobs, but Penny moved faster, wasn't tied up with so much red tape, and well, this was personal. Catching Archer studying their conversation, Elise moved along. "Why don't you tell Archer about the mask I sent you."

"Ah, the mask," Penny said, focusing on Archer. "I found a camera on it."

Archer's head cocked, eyes flared. "Where?"

"One of the gems." She jumped out of her seat and opened her filing cabinet with her fingerprint and then a code, and took out the mask. She returned with it in a bag, along with a small pouch that held the tiny circular camera.

Archer lifted the bag and studied the camera. "How did our bug scanner miss this?"

Penny shrugged. "It's very expensive, very new technology. I suspect your scanner is outdated."

Elise cringed at the flattening of Archer's lips. People were getting smarter. Technology was changing every day. Even Elise knew it was hard to keep up, and she had Penny who stayed on top of all of it. Archer finally asked Elise, "Could this camera have taken the photographs that were published in the tabloids?"

Elise looked to Penny for the answer.

Penny nodded. "I saw that article come out today, and most definitely. Nowadays, you can buy these cameras off Amazon, but the quality of your pictures suggests it's not a cheap knockoff."

Archer cursed, crossing his arms. "I suppose that's our confirmation then that Connie is behind this." Elise nodded in agreement, and Archer turned to Penny and asked, "I take it that Elise has updated you on our case."

Penny nodded, leaning back in her squeaking chair. "Here's what I got so far. You tell me if I'm right. Connie and Isaac used to date, but for whatever reason, Connie ended up marrying Isaac's older brother, Elijah. Now, Connie and Isaac both belong to a sex club where they don't have sex together but watch other people get it on, and Connie's husband isn't a member. Do I have that right?"

Archer nodded.

"Okay, and then Connie brings a camera into the club and snaps pictures of herself in the mirror, and proceeds to sell it to a tabloid. Right?"

"Yes," Archer confirmed.

"Weird," Penny said.

Archer gave a dry laugh. "Is that your final report?"

Penny laughed along with him. "For now. I'll dig into Connie and Isaac. Maybe they have money trouble and sold the photograph for that reason, but then how would they have the money to pay the Phoenix membership?" She glanced up at the ceiling, tapping her lip. "Weird."

Elise laughed. "Welcome to our headspace on this case. I'm going to keep looking into them on my end and see if anything comes up."

"Cool," Penny said. She reached for a blank notepad on her desk and wrote her phone number down, promptly offering it to Archer. "That's my secure number. If you'd like to get set up with me, instead of that shithead you use, call it. I'll tighten up that security of yours at the club."

Archer's gaze swung to Elise and held, and Elise shifted under the weight of that stare. She'd like to say she was helping Archer because it helped and protected Zoey and Rhys, but she would be a liar.

"Thank you," Archer said to Penny. "I'll definitely call."

"Great." Penny swatted at them. "Now go. I've got work to do."

As they turned away, Archer leaned down and asked, "Does she always dismiss you like that?"

"Always," Elise said with a grin.

Archer smiled. "I like her."

Elise figured he would. There was only one Penny in this world, and Elise was always glad to have her on her side.

Once they were back on the road, Archer asked, "So, where does this put us?"

"We're in what I call 'watch and wait,'" Elise said. "We need to let Penny do her job, and I'll do mine, and we wait to see if Connie and Isaac make another move."

Archer tapped his thumb against the steering wheel. "I could bring Connie in on the evidence of the camera in the mask alone. Scare her enough to make sure she doesn't make another move."

She believed he could put the fear in Connie. "But then you wouldn't know her motive. Yes, it may protect the club now, but maybe not in the future. My advice: wait to see what it is Connie and Isaac want, then bring the world crashing down around them."

He glanced her way again, and whatever he found in her expression made him nod. "All right, Elise, we'll do this your way."

She studied his relaxed posture and saw a shift there. They'd always played a pull-and-push game, but this wasn't that. He trusted her.

When they arrived home, Archer hung back as Elise went into her bedroom to change, many things running through his mind. He set his overnight bag down near the end of the couch, not liking the lack of answers, but he agreed with Elise's logic. They needed to see the bigger picture here before acting, and since Phoenix was closed for the time being, Connie and Isaac were distanced from the club. He liked to think they couldn't do more damage than they'd already done, but he never said never.

Elise returned to him a few minutes later, wearing joggers and a tight gray T-shirt that revealed she'd taken off her bra. She grabbed her laptop and made her way to the couch. He was tempted to skip talking and indulge himself to the tight peaks beneath her shirt, but curiosity got the better of him. After she dropped down next to him on the couch, powering up her computer, he said, "About Penny. Why would you share her with me if she's so good?"

Her fingers froze on the keyboard, but she lifted her gaze to him. "Why wouldn't I?"

"From my experience in this line of work, when someone gets someone good, they don't share."

She watched him closely for a moment, then lifted a

shoulder. "Penny is really good people, and the work she'll do for you would earn her big bucks. So, why wouldn't I help her?"

So Elise had a sweet side? Unexpected, but he liked it. Though her introducing Archer and Penny went above and beyond, especially considering the few PIs he knew weren't the sharing type. "How'd you get into private investigation?" he asked, curious about how such a woman came to fruition.

She snorted softly, throwing him a flat look. "I have no doubt you know everything about me, so don't you already know that?"

Also expected, but this was one thing she didn't know about him. "What I know of you is that you're a PI from Brooklyn who trained under Luke Hicks. That's as far as I dug."

Her head tilted to the side. "I hacked into your system. It's bad practice that you didn't dig more."

He laughed softly at her rebuke. "I had Wayne dig and get everything on you possible. It was my job to do just that."

"Then what happened?"

"Once I learned you didn't access anyone's private information at Phoenix and just got Zoey into the club, I didn't want to invade any more." Once he met her and felt that spark, he had wanted to learn about her the old-fashioned way.

She studied him, her eyes searching his before she addressed him again. "We're in total agreement. There are lines to cross, and there are some you don't." She sent him a dazzling smile. "I'm starting to realize there's something I like about you, Westbrook."

Heat spiraled down to his groin at the spark in that smile. He leaned in and lowered his voice. "I'd wager a bet I can name a few things you like about me, Fanning."

Her eyes dilated with her arousal, but she laughed it off. "Don't go getting a big head about it."

He laughed with her, swinging his arm on the back of the couch, behind her. "I'll try not to, but tell me, why a PI? Did you know Luke personally?"

She hesitated, like she questioned telling him the truth. Then her eyes went distant. "My father was a real scumbag. He beat the crap out of my mom for as long as I can remember, until one day he killed her."

"Jesus, Elise," Archer said, straightening in his seat. Whatever he thought she'd say, it certainly wasn't *that*. "Were you there when that happened?"

She gave a slight nod. "My mom hid me under the bed and told my father she'd told me to run. That obviously infuriated him. The bullets came after that."

Sickness rolled through him. "Was he arrested?"

"Nope," she said, with very little emotion. "He blew his brains out after calling in the murder."

Archer grabbed her thigh and was glad she let him. "Did you see that too?"

She went so very still, staring down at his hand on her thigh, and gave a small nod.

He became transfixed by the agony rippling across her features. "How old were you?"

"Six," she answered softly, finally meeting his gaze.

He noted a darkness there, deep pain. "Fuck, Elise," he said, his emotions in his throat. "I'm sorry that happened to you."

"Thanks," she said, with a slight shrug, brushing it off like what she said hadn't stopped the world from moving for a moment. "Luckily," she continued, her voice a little lighter now. "I was very little, and it's an amazing thing what the brain does with trauma. It puts it all in a box and files it away, letting a person move on."

He couldn't look away from her, and suddenly, Rhys' warning about being considerate, that maybe Elise isn't all strength and claws, made sense. Her past made Archer reassess her. To be so strong in the face of what she'd gone through, to help others to keep it from happening again... damn, she amazed him. "So, that's why you became a PI?"

"Exactly. I got into this to hunt scumbags before it ever gets bad enough that anyone gets hurt." She gave another little shrug. "I do a lot of pro bono work for the police, finding abusive husbands on the run."

"They're lucky to have your help."

Her gaze hit his again, and for the briefest moment, he saw softness he'd never seen before. It stole the air from his lungs. "I do what I can, so I can make sure what happened to my mom never happens again."

He nodded his response, not sure whatever he said would be the right thing. His first impression of Elise had always been that she was a smart, tough woman. But suddenly, his view shattered under her admission. She'd overcome so much, only making him want to know more. "Who raised you after your mother died?"

She gave a warm smile. "My aunt on my mom's side and my uncle. Both are grade-school teachers." She drew in a deep breath and shook her arms, obviously wanting to shake off the emotion. When she spoke again, she looked like the typical powerful Elise. "While the beginning of my life was rocky, after they took me in, they gave me stability and love." She jumped up, went over to the kitchen. "Hungry?"

"Always, can I help?"

"I've got it." She grabbed grapes out of the fridge and washed them. "All right, you got something from me. How about you—why did you leave the military?"

At that, he froze. "Shouldn't you know this about me too?

77

I have no doubt you dug into my life in retribution for digging into yours."

She laughed softly. "Sure, I considered it, but I didn't." She blotted the grapes dry with paper towels. "I have rules where it comes that too. Zoey told me about your military past."

He liked that they had that in common. "It wasn't one specific thing that had me retiring. It was a handful of things. It's a tough job, hard, relentless, disciplined, and it was almost an addiction. You trained and pushed harder to become stronger and better. I thrived on having a mission to carry out. But it takes a toll. One bad gunshot wound, hundreds of combat-related injuries, and your body eventually says no."

"That's the shot on your shoulder?"

He nodded. "Yeah." He stretched out his fingers, feeling the arthritis deep in his bones. "I thought I'd leave the military in a pine box, but when you're done, you're done. I couldn't have passed the testing again."

She grabbed a bag of almonds from the cabinet and poured some into a bowl. "That must have been a hard pill to swallow."

"It was. Took some adjustment to return to civilian life."

"So Rhys hired you as head of security for Phoenix?" she asked, returning to him with the two bowls and setting them on the coffee table.

"That's right. Rhys and I have been good friends for a long time now. He needed security, and I needed a job." He grabbed some grapes from the vines. "It's frustrating how hard it's been to do right by him and that job."

"Don't be too hard on yourself," Elise said, reaching for a handful of almonds. "The game is changing. The tech that's out there now is crazy. You just need a Penny. She'll get everything up to her standards at Phoenix."

"I appreciate it," he said, and he meant it. He ate a couple grapes, then asked, "All right, what's the plan now?"

"We'll give Penny til' the morning. She'll have something to move us in the right direction."

"Sounds like a good plan." Archer watched her eat the almonds, one by one, something shifting inside him. He'd brought Elise into this because he knew she was the best. Now, knowing the *why* that drove her changed things. Changed the way he saw her. Yeah, she liked to battle against him, strong and independent. But that's exactly what helped her survive.

She snorted a laugh and grabbed some grapes. "Why are you staring at me like that?"

He blinked, finding her watching him, eyes narrowed. "You're an amazing woman, Elise Fanning."

Her eyes widened, mouth falling open, then promptly shut.

The front door opened, and Hazel walked in, froze, then glanced between them.

Elise broke eye contact with Archer and said to Hazel, "Hey, don't look so surprised. You're the one who let him in here."

Hazel grinned, dark bags under her eyes. "Well, since he's not dead and I don't have to help you bury his body somewhere, I'm going to bed." She yawned and headed past them to her bedroom.

Elise popped the last grape into her mouth and rose. "It's late." She gave him a quick look, her emotions locked up tight. "Are you sure you're good here on the couch?"

"I've slept on the desert floor. This is good." He grabbed the small square pillow and placed it behind his head, wondering if he'd crossed a line Elise didn't want crossed. "Good night, Elise."

But the sweet smile she gave him told him she liked his

company. "Good night, Archer." She hit the light on her way out of the living room.

He took the blanket off the back of the couch, sliding it over him and then tucked an arm behind his head, listening to her footsteps pad their way down the hall to the bedrooms.

A door soon opened, and he smiled as Hazel said, "Tell me everything!"

a loud bang woke Elise from a dead sleep. She jolted up in bed, taking stock of her surroundings, her heart racing. The sun was shining outside, and her clock read 7:30 AM. She listened again, hearing more jostling coming from the living room. She quickly threw her hair up in a topknot, then opened her bedroom door, stepping out into the hallway in her strappy nightgown. In a few short strides, she spotted Archer in the kitchen, looking through the drawers. The coffeepot was pulled out from beneath the cabinets and the lid flipped open. "Coffee is in the cupboard next to the fridge."

He glanced back, looking unruffled from his sleep on the couch. "Did I wake you?"

"No," she lied, approaching him.

He gave an appreciative sweep of her in her nightgown, his eyes darkening before he went back to fixing the coffee. She headed for her cell phone, unsurprised to find a text. "Penny texted," she told Archer, sliding on the stool at the breakfast bar.

"What did she say?" He turned the coffeepot on.

Elise read the text quickly before giving him the shorter version. "That she's onto something but needs more time."

She texted back: TAKE ALL THE TIME YOU NEED. TALK SOON!

"That sounds promising," he said, turning around to lean against the counter.

She didn't mind waking up to Archer being in her kitchen. His hair was a little messy, his eyes slightly puffy, and his jeans and crisp white T-shirt made for one delicious package. "It does." She left her phone on the breakfast bar, then met him at the sink and grabbed two mugs from the cupboard. "Penny will get this figured out." She placed the mugs down, then took out the creamer and sugar. "We just have to wait her out."

"Good." His voice had lowered. She glanced over her shoulder, finding his focus on her ass. When he met her eyes again, he grinned. "That gives me time to do something else with you."

Heat pooled low in her body. "What's that?"

He had her in his arms a second later and planted a kiss on her mouth that did more for her adrenaline than any cup of coffee. When he broke away, he gave her butt a hard slap before releasing her. "You'll just have to wait and see."

The promise in that kiss stayed with her for the next two hours while they got ready, and they drove back into Manhattan to a gym in Soho, obviously one that catered to boxers. A ring was in the center of the room, but they skipped that and went to one of the corners where mats were placed in a large square.

"What exactly are we doing here?" Elise finally asked, turning in a circle, taking in the small gym. Free weights were on the right-hand side, a boxing bag on the other. A few men and women worked out near the free weights.

"You told me you can defend yourself," Archer explained, moving to the radio on the iPod station on the far side of the gym. When he turned back, hard rock music filled the room. "Show me."

"You're joking," she said, gaping at him.

He moved into the center of the mats and clapped his hands. "You have a dangerous job. I can help ensure you've got the skills to protect yourself. Let me see what you've got."

"I'm not doing this." She turned away, heading for the door.

He called after her, "I came to you for help because you're good at your job. I respect that about you. I'm good at protecting, defending, fighting. Respect that about me."

Dammit. She slowly turned back to him, spotted the intensity on his face, and it made her pause. Made her feel uncomfortable too. She was used to taking care of everyone else. Making sure everything was good and safe for them. She wasn't used to someone doing that for her. "It's not all that difficult to protect myself," she said, approaching him again. "I take my mace out and spray it, then run."

"Which works only if you have the time to grab your mace." He took a step closer. "What if I'm coming at you from the front?"

She grinned. "I'd kick you in the balls."

He gave a firm nod of approval. "Yeah, that's right. Hit hard. Get him on the ground."

"Want me to do that now, then?" she joked.

He laughed softly. "I think I'll pass on that." The laughter soon faded, and something about him shifted when he began talking. It occurred to her then that she was no longer looking at Phoenix's head of security; she was looking at the Green Beret.

Staying focused on his target—her—he moved even closer, charging the air around them. "If I get too close and kicking

83

isn't an option, go for the palm heel strike." He took her hand and lifted it. "Flex your wrist and aim for the nose. If you can't reach that, hit the throat as hard as you can."

"Okay," she said, feeling the heat of his touch leave her hand and circulate all over her body.

He lifted her elbow. "If you can't get enough momentum to throw a strong punch or kick, use your elbow and deliver a crushing blow to the face." She exhaled the breath she'd been holding as he moved in behind her, his strength at her back enveloping her. "If you get an attack from behind, you can get away with this same technique." He lifted her elbow again. "Eye your target. Pivot. And hit."

She swallowed deeply as he slid his hand down her arm, releasing her.

"Got it?"

"Yeah," she said, turning back to him, finding his smoldering gaze. Good, at least she wasn't the only one turned on one here.

He gave her a firm nod, waving her forward. "Let's try those out."

"Okay," she said, smiling to herself as she turned away. Sure, he'd taught her a few things, but she knew a few things too.

When he came at her from the front and attempted to wrap his arms around her, she snuck under them and then slid his feet out from under him. He landed on the mats on his back. Hard.

He burst out laughing. A laugh she'd never heard from him. So light and free, she could only laugh alongside him. He finally opened his eyes and leaned up on one arm. "Here I thought I was actually teaching you something. You know self-defense, then?"

"A little," she said. "Luke had me take a couple classes during my training."

"Why didn't you say anything?"

Because I didn't mind you touching me. "You seemed keen on teaching me," she said, instead.

His eyes sparkled with his chuckle as he jumped to his feet. "All right. Again?"

She smiled back, waving him forward this time. "Come at me."

And with a huge grin on his face, he did. Again and Again.

Until she landed hard on her back with him hovering over her. They were both breathing heavily from the exertion and dripping with sweat. She laughed freely, and he joined her, falling onto his back next to her. She'd had friends with benefits in her life before. Even had just guys as friends. But she realized now what she had with Archer was different. They'd both seen death up close and personal, and that created an understanding of sorts. They'd also both had to learn to fight in the world to make it safe. Catching her breath, she turned to face him, finding him already watching her. The laughter immediately faded to something...*more.*

She wasn't sure what she was thinking when she grabbed his face and kissed him, only that she knew she surprised him. But that surprise faded, and he quickly caught up, cupping her face and deepening the kiss.

By the time they broke away, she was near grinding herself into him. He brushed his nose against hers. "You told me you don't want to go to Phoenix again, but would you be open to a new adventure?"

Lost in the sizzling depths of his eyes, she asked, "What type of adventure?"

"Tonight I've been invited to a party of sensual indulgence."

Her brows rose. "So, it's like Phoenix?"

He shook his head. "No, it's among friends, not members. You can look at whoever you want to, or you don't have to look at all. We will be alone, no one watching. The choice is yours."

She examined him, looking for any hesitation on his face. She found none. "What if I say I don't want to?"

"Then we go back to your place tonight."

"You're okay with that?"

His brows rose. "Why wouldn't I be?"

She felt the insecurity roll through her but figured not talking about it would do her no good. "You have a very active life in the club. I don't, and even if I casually sleep with someone, I don't want someone's sloppy seconds. Won't you miss what you get at the club?"

He paused, seemingly choosing his words carefully. "Passion fuels my life. The club fulfills a need to give me that fix." He brushed his thumb against her bottom lip, giving her a sensual grin. "I find that fix with you too."

His solid nature and ability to share his thoughts was perhaps the sexiest thing about him. "So, you're not missing out."

His mouth twitched. "No, Elise, I'm most definitely not missing out on anything. So, what do you say?"

Settled by that, she considered his offer. She couldn't say she hated watching others; she simply didn't want them watching her. "I say yes."

LATER THAT AFTERNOON, Zoey called, inviting Elise and Hazel out for a night on the town with her and Rhys and his friends, Archer included. Archer indicated their hot night ahead of them wasn't happening until midnight. He'd spent the early afternoon at the cigar club, continuing to put out fires for Rhys, and Elise spent the day learning everything and anything on the internet about Connie and Isaac. Which didn't amount to much. Their lives seemed incredibly normal and privileged. When Hazel arrived at her office after work, they'd freshened up in the bathroom, and Elise slipped into skinny jeans, high heels, and a black silk blouse. Then they hopped in a cab and arrived at The Wicked Lion, a three-level bar in the East Village, where Elise found Archer, Zoey, Rhys, Kieran, and Hunt all sitting around a round table. The bar was packed full of customers, laughter and voices carrying over the air. Elise headed straight for the bar, ordering an Irish coffee martini from the bartender before she dared face the group. She needed some liquid courage.

The ground floor was a taproom, a traditional Irish pub that served draft beers and food. On the second floor was the parlor, where comfortable seating areas with photographs of old New York City littering the space. The top floor was an open canvas for music acts and special events.

As she reached the table, her world narrowed on Archer's sexy grin that was all for her. He rose and shocked her with a soft kiss on her lips. "Hi," he said, his voice low, before pulling out her chair for her.

"Hey." She smiled back, feeling the stares of everyone on her as she took the seat next to him. She refused to blush.

Blessedly, Archer, obviously reading her discomfort, broke the silence. "Anyone up for throwing some axes?" A few nights a week, the bar offered axe throwing on the third level.

Zoey and Hazel were grinning like fools at her because of Archer's obvious attraction toward her. Then she looked at Kieran and Hunt, unsure what she was expecting to find, but they surprised her. Kieran gave her a sweet smile, like he was simply saying hello. Hunt, a firm nod. In that one second, she realized Lottie had been right. This was very normal to them, and both Kieran and Hunt looked strong…and safe. She exhaled the breath she'd been holding. There was no judgment at this table.

"I've tried it," Hazel answered. "I can't even get the axe to stick in the wood."

Kieran barked a laugh. "You can't be that bad. I'll help you get it to stick."

Hazel blushed right up to her hairline. "It's okay. Truly, I really don't need to show anyone how really terrible I am at it. Thanks, but I'm good here."

Kieran winked at her. "Next time, then."

Hazel's blush darkened, and Elise fought her laughter. She'd never seen Hazel so frazzled before.

Next to Kieran was Hunt, who drained his beer. "I'm in."

Across from Elise were Zoey and Rhys, and Zoey shook her head. "I'll stay with Hazel."

All eyes came to Elise. "I'll pass on the first round. I'll play the winner." Elise hadn't seen Zoey or talked to her in the past few days, and she knew by her intense stare and big smile she sensed something had shifted between her and Archer. She needed to catch her up.

"I'll be that winner," Archer said with a smirk. He rose again, then brushed Elise's hair off her shoulder to plant a kiss there.

She fought off a shiver, trying to play it cool, even if he overheated her body.

"Bullshit," Hunt quipped, rising from his seat and pushing his chair back under the table. "You're going down."

"All talk," Kieran said, following them. "No game."

Rhys just shook his head at his friends, kissed Zoey, and then followed them up the stairs to the third level.

Elise smiled after them as folk music played through the speakers above the bar. She was really happy for Zoey, that she'd found love with Rhys, and she was glad for herself for how good things had been lately. She really liked this group of men. There simply wasn't any bullshit. They were solid, close, and she liked being around them.

When they vanished up the staircase, Elise turned to Hazel again, spotting her red cheeks. "You have really got to get your blushing under control around him."

She cringed. "I know. It's bad."

Zoey grasped the unopened wine bottle and popped the cork. "Why don't you ask him out?"

Hazel sputtered something incoherent before she managed, "Ask Kieran out?"

"Mm-hmm," Zoey replied, pouring wine from the bottle into a wineglass. "He's single, so why not?"

"No. God, no," Hazel said, shaking her head firmly. "Nope. Never going to happen."

"Why not?" Elise asked before taking a sip of her drink.

Hazel leaned in as if everyone could hear this conversation and the music didn't drown them out. "Because I honestly don't think I could survive him. Look at me, I can't stop blushing like a teenage girl, and he's not even saying anything dirty."

Elise swallowed her sip and waggled her eyebrows. "Do you want him to say something dirty?"

Hazel's face turned a deep shade of red. "Please stop."

Elise laughed; Zoey did too, until the laughter faded away. Elise asked, "In all seriousness, what's your hang-up here?"

"I'm not like you guys," Hazel said.

Zoey exchanged a long look with Elise, then frowned at Hazel. "How so?"

"Sensual. Erotic. Experienced. All of it," Hazel said. "You know my past." And that past was painful for Hazel. Hazel's ex-boyfriend had done a real number on her heart, including taking her virginity and then dumping her the next day. Hazel hadn't dated since. "I'm...yeah, no, I just can't." Coming from a terrible mother didn't help Hazel's confidence either. Elise had only heard a fraction of the stories, and the emotional abuse Hazel received at the hands of her rich mother was awful.

Elise actually understood. Zoey likely did too. Sometimes fear got the better of a person. "Well, then, just keep on blushing," she told Hazel.

Zoey agreed with a firm nod, grinning. "And late at night, when you're in bed all alone, grab your favorite battery-operated lover and think about him then."

"Oh my God, Zoey," Hazel breathed, covering her face with her hands, nearly melting into her seat.

Elise let her off the hook and put the spotlight on herself. "So, I guess you're wondering what's going on with Archer and me."

Zoey nodded frantically. "That's a big yes."

"Please, yes, let's talk about you," Hazel said, reaching for her cosmopolitan.

"We're not serious," Elise reported. "So, don't go thinking that things are going that way. We're very comfortable in the friends-with-benefits category."

Zoey lifted her eyebrows. "He kissed you twice since you showed up."

Elise shrugged. "He's...touchy."

Zoey's mouth twitched. "I'm sure he is."

She hesitated, and Elise knew that measured look. "What is it?"

"Well, I've seen you be in a friends-with-benefits situation before, and I don't know. This seems like more."

Hazel raised her hand. "I second that."

Elise took a sip of her drink, tasting the hint of vanilla,

and pondered. "I'm not going to say I don't like him. I do. He's a good guy; actually, I think he's the best guy I've ever met."

"He's also hot," Hazel added.

"And hot," Elise agreed. "What we have is just intense. You know how it goes. Eventually, that will fizzle out, and we'll be done."

"Or maybe something else will grow from the chemistry," Zoey said.

Elise pointed at Zoey. "Don't go putting things like that in my head. You know how I feel about relationships."

"Yeah, yeah, I know," Zoey grumbled, running her fingers up and down the stem of her glass. "All I'm saying is, would it really be so bad if you did get serious with someone?"

"Yes," Elise said. "Because what I know of relationships and marriage is abuse from my own family and horrible cheating through my work. I see people at their worst every day, and I know what's possible. I don't need a big commitment to be happy. Things are good. Why change that?"

Zoey said, "Well, yes, some relationships are bad, but not every relationship is like that. What Rhys and I have isn't terrible."

"No, it's not," Elise said with a nod. "But you're also you. You're good at that love stuff. I'm not. I don't know how to be."

Hazel jumped in and said, "I'm with Elise on this one. You and Rhys make it look easy. You mesh really well. It's not like that for everyone."

Zoey watched them both closely, like she knew secrets they didn't, and finally offered, "I hope you two find *easy* then, in whatever way makes you happy."

Done with the serious talk, Elise added, "Or we find multiple orgasms with total hunks."

Zoey burst out laughing. "Or that."

Glad to have her best friends caught up in her life, she lifted her drink to her mouth right as Archer came trotting down the stairs, grinning from ear to ear.

"You're up," he said to Elise when he reached the table.

She rose, taking her drink with her. "I take it that means you won?"

"Did you have any doubt?" he asked with an arched brow.

"Yes."

He snorted and slapped her ass. Deliciously hard. "Smart-ass." Then he headed for the staircase.

She smiled after him, relishing the heat on her bottom, which quickly faded as a snicker sounded behind her. She glanced back, discovering Zoey's and Hazel's grins.

"Is that something friends do to each other?" Zoey asked. "Hazel, bend over."

Elise quickly gave her the finger, sending Hazel and Zoey into a fit of laughter before she followed Archer up the staircase. When she reached the top, taking in the rows of wood boards with bull's-eyes painted onto them, she noticed the guys down at the bar ordering another drink.

"Before we start our game, you'll need this for tonight," Archer said, handing her a business card.

The card was a simple shiny black business card with bold gold letters that read: MIDNIGHT DREAMS. "What's this?"

"Your ticket into the party tonight." He gave her a sensual smile. "I'll have a driver pick you up at eleven-thirty. Keep that card with you. You'll need it to gain entrance."

She studied the card again. It revealed nothing, but excitement fluttered in her belly. She couldn't deny, though, the erotic games fueled something unknown inside her. "What is the attire?"

Desire danced in his eyes, and she burned in response to it. "The driver will have what you need."

Her fingers began to tingle, and that feeling soon spiraled down low in her body. "All right, so what now?"

His grin was hot and wicked. "I kick your ass at throwing axes."

"Dream on," she purred. "Your ass is toast."

9

Once Elise kicked his ass at axe throwing, Archer dropped her and Hazel off at the subway station and made his way over to Rhys' place. Tonight's festivities weren't starting until midnight, and they had some time to kill. Poker was a regular thing for Friday night, so he'd come with a six-pack of beer. While he felt each passing minute with painful slowness, anticipating a fun night ahead, he was glad for something to keep his mind busy before he'd see Elise again, wearing the outfit he'd chosen for her. He knew she was pushing her limits for him, and while he appreciated it, he planned to show her how he wasn't missing out on anything by not spending his nights at the club or sleeping with strangers. In his youth, he'd gotten off on the eroticism of different women; now he hungered for something more. A deeper connection. Something he was finding with Elise.

Sitting at a poker table set up in Rhys and Zoey's living room, Rhys began shuffling the cards and asked Archer, "Tell me if it's none of my business, but how are things going with Elise?"

Archer expected the question after he'd kissed Elise, not

once, but twice today. These men were his family. They knew everything about his past and present. "It's good."

Hunt finished the sip of his beer and shook his head. "I'm honestly surprised you two have not killed each other."

Next to Hunt, Kieran snorted a laugh. "They're too busy fucking each other's brains out to worry about killing each other."

"It's intense," Archer agreed. "She's intense. It's unlike anything I've ever experienced before with anyone."

Rhys began dealing the cards. "Do you think anything serious will come of it?"

"I'm not sure," Archer replied honestly, waiting for the cards to be dealt before picking them up. "She's been very up front about not wanting a relationship. I'm not pushing it. We're enjoying each other and having fun."

"Sometimes, it's good to let this happen organically," Rhys said as he finished dealing.

Especially with Elise, was what Rhys hadn't said. Now Archer knew what he was working with. Funnily enough, her past would have sent him running at one point in his life. She came with some pretty heavy baggage, and starting anything serious with her would not come easy for him, but he didn't want to run. He wanted to stay. "If I tried to push Elise into something, I've got no doubt she'd gut me."

Laughter filled the room. To get the focus off him, he shot Kieran a look. "How about we talk about what you're doing with Hazel?"

Kieran snorted, sorting his cards. "There's nothing to discuss. I'm not doing anything with her."

"Bullshit," Hunt quipped. "She likes you, and you know it."

"I like making her blush," Kieran countered, reaching for his beer and taking a long sip. "What's wrong with that?"

"Not a damn thing." Hunt picked up his cards and began sorting them. "If you weren't lying to yourself."

Kieran punched him in the arm, sending Hunt into a fit of laughter. "I'm not lying to myself," Kieran shot back. "Hazel is cute, and I'm enjoying teasing her, but she's…"

"Innocent," Rhys offered.

"Exactly," Kieran agreed. "She's too innocent. I wouldn't even know what to do with that." He settled his beer back down in the drink holder on the poker table. "I'm having fun with her. That's all."

Hunt grinned. "Might be more fun corrupting her."

"No," Kieran said firmly.

There was something dark in the way he said no that had Archer examining him a little closer. And he wasn't the only one. Rhys cocked his head, studying Kieran too. Something heavy was going on there, between Kieran and Hazel, Archer would bet all his poker chips on it.

The thought faded away when Zoey entered the room, carrying bowls of tortilla chips and salsa, and set them on the table. "Thanks, love," Rhys said, bringing her on his lap and giving her a long kiss.

"You're welcome. Are you winning?"

"No," Rhys grumbled. "Maybe you should take over."

"Yeah, right, I'll lose all our money. I know nothing about poker." She cupped Rhys' face again and gave him a quick kiss. "Besides, I need to go get ready for tonight. Have fun."

Archer watched them, happy for them—Rhys deserved all the happiness in the world—and what they had seemed so easy, so healthy. He wondered what that would be like. To have a woman to wake up to every day. To have a sidekick. He shook the thought from his head and asked Rhys, "How are the wedding plans coming along?"

"Good," Rhys said, looking at his cards. "We're thinking of a fall wedding."

"Nice," Hunt said. "Not too hot. You won't sweat your balls off in a suit."

"My thoughts precisely." Rhys smiled and then told the group, "We should have a date for you soon."

Archer just nodded, focusing back on his shit cards, knowing he wouldn't win this hand.

Continuing to sort his cards, Hunt asked, "How's the case going?"

There had never been secrets between this group. Phoenix was home to them all. The safe haven to play and indulge in their wickedest fantasies alongside the men Archer would give his life to protect. Obviously, Rhys had let them in on the happenings at the club. "It's slow going, but I'm pretty confident we'll find out what Connie and Isaac are up to," Archer explained.

"That's all I can ask," Rhys said with a smile, taking some weight off Archer's shoulders. "We've lost a total of seven members, but I expect three will come back once we can prove this matter is resolved."

Kieran whistled. "What a fucking mess they caused. I got lucky that no one could identify me with my mask."

Archer nodded in agreement.

Hunt began talking more about his thoughts on the case, but Archer didn't make out the words as he caught Zoey standing in the doorway, waving at him.

He gave her a quick nod and listened as Hunt said, "Just let me know if you need police intervention. I can help, if you need me."

"Thank you. I'll reach out if I need to." Archer rose, placing his cards face down on the poker table. "Let me take a piss before we start." He headed out of the kitchen and into the hallway where the bathroom was located.

At the end of the corridor, Zoey waited by the bathroom door. "Everything okay?" he asked.

She folded her arms. "She likes you. You know that, right?"

He lifted an eyebrow at her. "Are we talking about Elise?"

"Yes, of course," Zoey said, her cheeks stained a bit red. "I know this is totally none of my business, but well, Elise is my best friend, and I just don't want you to miss anything."

He blinked at her. "What am I missing?"

Zoey unfolded her arms and then folded them again, barely able to stand still. "I've never seen her the way she is with you. She's...happy."

He wasn't seeing the problem here. "Isn't that a good thing?"

"It would be if you were both on the same page," Zoey said. She hesitated, then lifted her chin. "Rhys told me you haven't really had any serious relationships, and that's fine and everything, just not when—"

"It comes to your best friend," he finished for her. He hadn't dated seriously back in the military because of being deployed, but he also hadn't met anyone he wanted more with. Until Elise.

Zoey relaxed a smidgen with her nod. "So, all I'm saying is, please be careful. She means everything to me, and well, it's really nice to see her happy."

Archer cupped Zoey's shoulder, a move he'd do with any family. "I won't hurt her, if that's what you're asking, Zoey. I know Elise is important to you. If at any time, Elise doesn't want what is happening between us, it stops, just like that."

Zoey paused. "But what if she wants more?"

"Has she told you that?"

"No, but—"

Archer smiled as softly as he could. "I'm not sure if you've spoken to Elise lately about this, but she's made it very clear how she feels about relationships."

"I know, it's just..."

"You care about your friend?" Archer offered.

Zoey sighed. "I do."

"Don't worry." Archer squeezed her shoulder again. "Rhys has already asked me to be careful with her feelings, and I promise that I will be. She's running the show here." He smiled. "I'm just along for the ride. All right?"

"Okay," Zoey hedged, the rest of the tension leaving her face. "Don't think I don't really like you, because I do."

"Stop. I know your heart is in a good place. This is all good, Zoey. Promise."

Finally, she smiled. "You're right; it is a good thing, and I'm very happy for you two, that you're having fun together."

His own smile fell as he left Zoey behind and he headed back toward the poker table. Elise's words and her emotions didn't line up. Even Zoey confirmed that. Sure, Archer got that fear built up roadblocks, but he felt himself become unsteady with his next steps. Did Elise want more? Was she just scared? Was he giving her enough? Was he truly ready to go all in with her?

~

"GOOD EVENING, MS. FANNING," the dark-haired driver said the moment Elise left the loft and met him outside at eleven-thirty sharp. He wore an all-black suit, looking like a security guard and not a driver.

Maybe Phoenix security? "Good evening," she said, wearing the same outfit she was in earlier, but she'd freshened up her makeup, and Hazel had helped curl her hair in big waves.

He opened the back seat door for her. "There's a box there for you."

"Thank you," she said, sliding into the leather seat of the Mercedes.

He shut the door behind her, and she noticed there was a privacy divider separating her and the driver. She heard his door shut and the engine start before she reached for the rectangular box next to her. When she lifted the lid, she breathed, "Wow."

She took out the stunning Venetian metal gold-and-black masquerade mask with a black ribbon. The weight of it, the intricate details, it was the most beautiful mask she'd ever seen in her life. It occurred to her then that Archer had picked this specifically for her tonight, and to know he was likely fantasizing about her in this outfit, only made it all the more special. She set the mask aside, pulling out exquisite black lace lingerie with matching thong, garter belt, and stockings. The sudden throb between her thighs had her squeezing her legs together for friction. She wasn't sure what that said about her that one look at this lingerie turned her on, but she wasn't overthinking it either. Beneath the lingerie were black stilettos and a long black trench coat. And at the very bottom was a tube of dark-red lipstick.

"We're about fifteen minutes away, Ms. Fanning," the driver said over the speakers.

"Okay, thank you." The intercom clicked off, and Elise set to undressing and redressing in the lingerie.

By the time they rolled to a stop and the driver turned off the car, Elise was just finishing applying the lipstick using the camera on her phone as a mirror. She quickly rubbed her lips together, giving herself a quick look in the camera, not even recognizing herself. While she didn't get a great look at the lingerie on her, she felt sexy. Far sexier than ever before. And the mask plus the lipstick...*God, who am I?* She set the lipstick down and tied her coat shut right as the driver opened the door.

He held out his hand, and as she took it, climbing out of the car, she also took in the mansion he'd brought her to. "Where are we?" she asked him.

He gave a knowing smile. "I'm afraid I cannot give out that information, ma'am." He gestured her forward, releasing her hand. "Please enjoy your evening. I'll be waiting for you here when you'd like to go home."

"Thank you."

As he headed back to the car, she moved toward the grand porch steps where warm lights greeted her, as well as a security guard with an ear communicator in his ear.

"Your pass, please?" he asked.

She hesitated, but then remembered the card Archer had given her earlier. She took it from her purse and offered it.

He scanned the card with a black light, obviously looking for a symbol she didn't know was there, then he opened the door, pocketing the card. "Enjoy your night."

"I suspect I will." She smiled and entered the mansion, feeling like she did not belong there one bit. Whoever owned the place was loaded, and not just a little, but stinkin' rich. Marble covered the floors. A grand staircase of old hardwood led to the upstairs. Fancy art decorated the walls. A pleasant scent of potpourri carried through the space. Not a spot in this house wasn't thought about and decorated to showcase the wealth of the owners.

"May I take your coat?" a tall shirtless man wearing only dress slacks asked.

"Sure, thank you." She undid the buckle, then slid out of the coat and handed it to him.

He gave her a long look over, appreciation in his eyes. Apparently, Archer chose her lingerie just right. "Please let me know if you need anything tonight," he said before turning away.

She nearly called after him to ask him what she was supposed to do now, when a sensual moan came from her left. She moved in that direction, entering a sitting room, finding a couple in a hot sixty-nine position while a few others watched. None were Archer. They paid her no attention, so she paid them none either, walking to the next room. She passed a waiter, taking a champagne glass as she went. Her heels clicked against the marble floor as she spotted a pool table, where a woman was pleasuring another woman with her mouth. She realized this wasn't like Phoenix in the way people watched. This was more...*intimate.* Playful, even.

Moving along, she strode by one room, where a crowd had gathered. But seeing long strawberry-blonde hair, she quickly looked away and moved along. She'd recognize that hair anywhere. Zoey. And the black-haired man she rode with earnest was without a doubt Rhys. An odd sensation followed. Not arousal; it just never came. But a peculiar sense of happiness for Zoey. She was living her life, sensually and alive, and while Elise had no intention of watching them, she also didn't feel as perturbed as she had thought she would.

Every room she passed had more people, more sex, more eroticism, and it tickled across her flesh as she made her way down a hallway. A quick look outside, and she saw Archer, wearing his black slacks and a black mask and nothing else. Heat and need drove her to open the door and go to him.

The second he saw her, he rose. She saw the flex of his hands, the way his eyes followed her every move.

"When I picked that outfit for you," he said. "I thought you'd look beautiful, but Elise, goddamn it, you look fucking stunning."

"Thank you," she said, scanning over the hard line of his jaw, his sculpted chest to his six-pack. She wanted her hands on all of him, and her mouth. "You just make me hungry."

"Well, then, let's get you fed." His mouth twitched as he took her hand and then led her down a pathway that opened to a gorgeous spa oasis. The kidney-shaped hot tub was surrounded by large boulders and greenery, making her feel like she'd stepped into a natural hot spring. Next to the hot tub was a beach bed with long white drapery blowing in the slight breeze.

"We're alone out here," Archer said, drawing her gaze back to him. "No one will watch you tonight."

She gestured back to the house. "There's quite a few shows going on in there."

"There are, and I wanted you to see that," he said. "Because an erotic atmosphere turns you on."

"How do you know that?" she asked with a soft laugh.

A sly smile crossed his face as he closed the distance, slipping a finger inside her panties, then dragging it across her silkiness. "This sweet, drenched cunt is how I know."

Heat burned at his bold word choice, causing her nipples to tighten. The hunger in his eyes washed over her, and she couldn't help herself. She pressed on his chest, and his finger slipped from inside her. Amusement danced in his eyes as she kept on pushing until his legs hit the bed. Keeping her eyes on his, she opened his pants and slid her hands over his ass as she lowered them to the ground, where they hit his bare feet.

"I want to taste you," she told him.

His devilish smile greeted her as he sat down on the bed, his legs wide, his big, beautiful cock hard and ready for her.

She went to her knees, grabbed his impressive length, and dragged her tongue up from the base all the way to the tip. His low groan hit her like the best kind of foreplay. She kept looking at him, watching the way he reacted as she circled her tongue around the tip, feeling his deep shudder. Another swirl later, and she slid her tongue against the slit, drawing the pre-cum into her mouth, savoring the taste of him, the musky scent. Then she devoured him, relishing his guttural groan. His hand threaded into her hair as she began to bob on him.

"Eyes on me."

She looked at him, staying on the tip, sucking there.

"Fucking Christ, woman," he growled. "You could make me come just by looking at me like that."

A second later, she found herself gathered in his arms and up on her knees on the bed. He reached for the condom wrapper waiting on the bed, and after he sheathed himself, his grip held tight on her hips as he pulled her ass closer to him and slapped her. Hard. She shivered and moaned, and he took that as his invitation to move her panties aside and plunge forward, all the way to the hilt.

She lost awareness of anything but how he was in charge of her. Every move was his to command. Every scream ripped from her body, he owned. Until *he* became so overwhelming, filling her completely, wonderfully, that she was panting, out of control from the pleasure.

Another hard slap on her ass, followed by his hand fisting her hair. He pulled her head back until he growled in her ear. "Come with me, Elise."

Another slap.

She gasped.

Another slap.

"Fuck, yes," she screamed.

His answering deep groan followed before he gripped her hips tight, pounding her from behind, hard and fast, until all the tension exploded into waves of never-ending pleasure.

10

*E*lise ate a quick breakfast the next morning, grabbed two to-go coffees, then hopped on the subway and headed over to Penny's place, the entire time thinking about her night with Archer. Last night, they'd gone in the hot tub twice and had sex four more times in that backyard oasis. She liked the eroticism and feeling sexy, but if she hadn't been with Archer, she wondered if she'd feel the same way. Her head was foggy with it all. And when she shifted in her seat, sensing the warm wetness between her thighs, she refocused on the task ahead of her. Archer said he had meetings and work to catch up on at Phoenix, and Elise wanted to move forward with the case. So they'd parted ways with a bone-melting kiss Elise couldn't stop thinking about this morning. When she arrived at Penny's a little after nine o'clock, her friend buzzed her inside quickly.

"No hottie today?" Penny asked by way of greeting, stretching out her arms.

Elise handed her a coffee. "Sadly, not today." She grabbed the empty swivel chair and took a seat next to Penny's desk. "He's got work to do, and so do we."

105

"Yes, we do." Penny lifted her paper cup with a wide smile. "Thanks for this. I think I got a total of two hours of sleep last night."

A quick survey of Penny revealed dark circles under her eyes and hair that looked like it needed a washing. "I take it that means you've found something."

"Okay, first, let me update you on your break-in. The cops have a hit on the prints. I'm still waiting for their report to hit their system and then I'll let you know what develops."

"Awesome, thank you," Elise said. "Do you think it's connected to Connie and Isaac?"

"My gut tells me no, but I've been wrong before, so let's wait and see what happens."

"Sounds good."

The whir and buzz of the old pipes filled the air as Penny took a long sip of her coffee. "And to answer your question, I did find something on our case." She set her coffee down and turned her chair to face her monitors and began typing on her keyboard. "I put some focus on Connie and Isaac's relationship. From what I've found so far, Connie and Isaac were a thing back in college."

Photos popped up on one of her computer screens, showing a happy couple, looking very much in love. "Do you know when they broke up?"

Penny clicked a few more buttons on her keyboard, and more photographs flashed on the monitors. "Looks like a year after college. After that, there's a two-year span when their lives seem to go in two different directions. Interestingly, Isaac ends up in Las Vegas and gets into big-money poker."

Elise sipped her coffee, catching the notes of hazelnut in the brew. "Bet his oil-tycoon daddy loved that."

"Right?" Penny agreed with a nod. "Looks like he blew through a million before daddy forced him into rehab."

A photograph of Isaac popped up on the screen. He was smiling from ear to ear, his arms slung over the shoulders of two others, all wearing casual white clothes with HOPE RECOVERY CENTER written on the chest of their T-shirts. "Did Isaac come back to Manhattan after rehab?"

Penny nodded. "Looks like it." She typed on her keyboard again. "About six months after Isaac came back, Connie married his brother."

Photographs of their gorgeous wedding replaced the rehab photos. Connie wore a stunning mermaid lace gown. "She looks happy."

"Yeah, she does."

Elise took another sip of her coffee, pondering. "If we look at this from the outside, maybe it's as simple as things with Isaac didn't work, and he introduced Connie to his brother."

Penny agreed with a nod. "Totally plausible." She studied the photograph of Connie feeding her husband a piece of wedding cake. "But why would two exes end up at an exclusive, expensive sex club together without that brother?"

"It's odd," Elise hedged. "The whole thing just doesn't feel right. Their behavior was definitely off that night I saw them. Now there is this connection. And the fact that she's obviously the one who sold the photograph of her and Isaac to the tabloids." Her instincts were raising all the alarms, but the dangling piece to pull all this together simply wasn't there.

"Even more odd," Penny said as numerous photographs of Connie and Isaac popped up on the screen, "is that Connie paid to have her ties with Isaac buried."

Elise blinked. "Pardon me?"

Penny's eyes crinkled with amusement. "Yeah, that was my reaction too. At first, I couldn't find anything on them as a couple. Sometimes that's not surprising, especially if they're not on social media, but when I say I couldn't find anything, I mean I couldn't find *anything*. No phone calls. No texts. Nothing."

"So, you looked deeper?"

Penny grinned. "Exactly." More banging on her keyboard, then phone records and text messages popped up on the screen. "Just so happens, the hacker Connie hired is someone I know. I made a call and found out that, about the time Isaac returned to Manhattan was when Connie paid a hacker to bury everything." Her smile widened. "Of course, nothing digital is actually buried forever."

"That's a terrifying thought," Elise admitted. "But good for us."

"Great for us, actually." She turned away from her monitor again, picking up her coffee cup. "I'll save you from reading all the messages like I did, but I can tell you without any doubt in my mind that Connie and Isaac are hopelessly and madly in love."

Elise gave her head a shake, trying to knock sense into it. "But she's married to his older brother."

"Exactly," Penny drawled. "Like I said before, weird."

Elise considered everything she'd heard, coming to one conclusion. "They're up to something."

"I'd bet my money on it," Penny agreed before sipping her coffee. "My gut tells me this doesn't have anything to do with Phoenix. There's been nothing else put out in the media, no more whispers of secret, naughty sex clubs. Nothing."

"And they haven't blackmailed Rhys," Elise said.

Penny nodded in agreement.

Elise set her coffee down, running her hands over her face. "These people are so fucking weird. Honestly, I've never had so much trouble piecing a case together. It's like every direction you look, something doesn't add up." She dropped her hands, pondering her next steps. Most cases, Elise could handle from a distance, but sometimes she needed to get closer to get a better feel for the people she was investigating. "Can you get me a meeting with Isaac?"

Penny lifted an eyebrow. "What sort of meeting?"

"Any kind," Elise said, rising. "I want to meet him. See if anything comes of that. Feel what kind of guy he is. I need to get into their headspace, and sitting around, waiting to see if they act again, isn't working."

"Isaac seems to be into some new startups," Penny said, turning back to her monitors. "Shouldn't be too hard to set up some kind of meeting with him if we say you're an investor. Let me find out what companies he's involved with and get you that information. Tomorrow good for a meeting?"

"That'll do," Elise said. "Shoot me the details when you've got them."

"Will do. What's your plan now?"

Elise pushed her chair back in the corner where she'd found it. "I'll spend the day following Connie. See what kind of life she leads."

"Let me know if anything comes of that."

"You know I will. Thanks, girl."

She headed for the door when Penny said, "Oh, and I also did a little digging on that boy toy of yours."

Elise turned back with a frown. "One, I never asked you to do that. And two, he's not my boy toy."

Penny waggled her eyebrows. "Sure looked like it by the way he looks at you. Want to know what I found?"

"No, I don't." Not only did she never look into her friends' lives, but she wasn't sure she even wanted to know. If he had something bad in his history, it would shape her opinion of him. And she happened to like her opinion of him right now. Especially her opinion of their sex together. "But thanks for looking out for me."

Penny lurched off her chair, grabbing a large envelope

before hurrying to Elise's side. "Normally, I wouldn't push these things, but there is something in here you should see."

Elise rolled her eyes, taking the envelope. "It's going in the trash unopened, Penny."

"Do with it what you will," Penny said, wiggling her fingers in a wave before heading back to her desk. "All I'm saying is if I were you, I'd look inside."

Elise felt the weight of the envelope, meaning whatever was inside had paperwork written up about it. Elise trusted Penny, and she knew she wouldn't have given the information without due cause. But really, only one thing truly mattered. "Am I in danger with him?"

Penny dropped back into her chair. "That depends on your definition of danger."

"You do realize that's not helpful at all," Elise pointed out.

Penny grinned. "I know."

ARCHER RETURNED to Elise's later that night, exhausted. Not being at Phoenix constantly meant he had to catch up on everything he had missed. He'd spent his entire day in meetings, and he'd packed three days of work into one. And weighing on all of that was the awareness that he was nowhere closer to finding out why Connie and Isaac had published that damn photograph. He parked in front of the loft and cut the ignition, running a hand across the ache stretching across the back of his neck. Knowing Elise could break the tension running through him, he opened his truck's door when his cell phone rang. *Mom* popped up on the screen. She called every couple of weeks, probably would call more if she hadn't met Gerry, her husband of ten years now. He hit the speakerphone. "Hi, Mom."

"Hi, honey. How are you?"

Her warm voice was like a weighted blanket across his chest. He leaned his head back against the headrest. "Long day, but doing good."

"So happy to hear it. Is Rhys busy, then?"

His mom knew what she had to know. That Archer worked for Rhys as head of his security—she'd met him when she came to New York City—but she didn't know the security was for a secret sex club. Considering all of Archer's missions in the past had been top secret, he surmised his mother figured Rhys had some ties to that. "He's busy; therefore, I'm busy too. How's traveling going?"

"Oh, it's just so wonderful," said his mom, her voice holding a whimsical tone. "We took a train from Barcelona to Paris a few days ago. Long ride, but so worth it. You must come to Paris sometime. The food, the people, the history, it's all amazing."

"I'm sure it is. How's Gerry?"

"Loving every minute of this trip," she answered. "We both are."

Archer shut his eyes, relishing in the happiness in his mother's voice. For so long, she'd struggled. His father was deployed just after Archer turned one year old. He died during active service. His mother paid the price. She'd worked at a diner for as long as he could remember. Her wage plus tips simply wasn't enough. She'd worked two jobs his whole childhood in order to raise him, so when he was old enough, he took care of her. Seeing that he didn't need much money during his deployment, except a little for clothes and food, he sent the rest to his mother. Until Gerry came along. He was a stockbroker who fell in love with the waitress. He'd swept her off her feet and gave her the life she deserved. Archer respected and liked him. More importantly, he appreciated the happiness Gerry brought his mother. "Where are you off to next?" Now that Gerry was retired, they spent their time traveling the world. "We're staying here in Paris for a little while. There's just so much to see."

"You'll send pictures?"

"Of course." His mother paused. "I hope you're not working all the time and having fun too."

She was digging for information on his personal life. He went to answer, oddly surprised he wanted to tell her about Elise. "I don't work that hard, and yes, I'm having fun."

"Good. Glad to hear it." Another pause. "Okay, sure, I'm coming," his mother said to someone else in the room with her. "I have to run. We've got a tour planned this afternoon. I miss and love you."

"Love you, too. Goodbye."

"Bye, honey."

The phone line went dead, and Archer shoved his cell back into his pocket, finally exiting his truck. He had never spoken about any woman to his mother, and she knew better than to pester him about it. She'd like Elise. Her directness. Her steel-like strength where it came to Archer and her smart mouth. He'd seen his mother suffer, and that's why he never got serious with anyone until he could be there for her fully. Like Gerry was there for his mother. It occurred to him then that he wanted that with Elise. To show her not all relationships were bad. That some were incredible. To show her what was possible. The thought warmed something cold in his chest as he made it up to the loft and knocked on the door.

A moment later, it opened to Hazel. "Hi," she said with a warm smile. "Still staying with us?"

He nodded. "A little bit longer, if that's okay."

"Of course," she said, opening the door a little wider. "You're the one making sure we're safe. I'd be silly not to be grateful for that."

He smiled at her appreciation, removing his shoes at the door. "Is Elise here?"

"Yeah, she's in the shower. Go on in to her room."

"Thanks."

Spicy hints lingered in the air as he strode through the loft, indicating the women had already eaten dinner. Archer had grabbed a sub on the way out of Manhattan. Something akin to happiness touched his chest when he headed down the hallway. For all the shit hanging over him at the club, things felt good. Easy. He had no doubt it all had to do with Elise. These past days with her felt...*perfect.* The thought stayed with him until he entered her bedroom, finding the space decorated in a way that reflected the woman herself—smart with thick and sturdy bedroom furniture that was built to last and decorated with warm colors.

On her queen-sized bed, there was a large envelope. The front read: Hottie Boy Toy. It didn't take much to know whatever was in this envelope was about him. He took a seat on the side of the bed and picked up the envelope, feeling the weight of it.

His past. There it was in a single envelope.

He heard a creak ahead of him and glanced up to find Elise standing in the doorway wearing nothing but a towel, her hair dripping water down her arms. "You could have just asked me, if you wanted to know about my past," he told her.

She closed the door behind her, then shook her head. "I didn't ask Penny to look into you. She handed me the envelope this morning."

He lifted an eyebrow at her. "But you didn't destroy it?"

"No, but I also left it out so you'd see it."

"Why?"

"Because Penny wouldn't have given it to me if she didn't think I needed to see something." Her steady gaze held his as she came to sit next to him on the bed. "So, tell me, what do I need to know?"

"You didn't look inside?"

Again, she shook her head. "I told you, I don't do that."

He drew in the longest breath of his life, then gestured to the envelope. Going into the past wasn't easy. He'd left it behind for a reason. To live a civilian life without being haunted by the darkness war brought. "Open it."

"I don't need to," she said, adamant.

"I want you to," he said, and he meant it, offering her the envelope.

She hesitated but then must have trusted that he did want this, since she took the envelope and opened it. He looked down at the contents first and then wished he hadn't.

His heart sank into his gut, his mind yanking him away from Elise and taking him to a place he hadn't gone in a long time.

Gunshots rang out through the dark night.

"Westbrook, you've got your orders. Get the target and get the fuck out."

His legs ached to book it at the command issued to him. The training running through his veins, his instincts fighting to obey the order. And yet, the little girl screaming, with tears rushing down her cheeks while she stood shaking near the stone pillar. Her mother had already been taken by Archer's team to safety. Intel never mentioned a child. A child caught in the middle of a war she was born into.

So scared. So alone. *He hit his ear communicator. "I will not leave her. Cover me."*

Roars from countless voices followed him as he charged forward. He felt the first punch to his shoulder and quickly took aim, firing toward the gunman on his right. The next bullet soared by him; another one followed. He heard the gunfire behind him, one of his brothers taking out that threat. Another blow hit the ground ahead of him as he dove toward the little girl and she leapt in the safety of his arms.

"You refused to leave the little girl there?"

Archer snapped back into focus, his gut heavy, his hands clammy as he fought the chill in his veins. "The order was to extract the mother and keep her safe until she could testify against her husband. The child wasn't supposed to be there. Our intel suggested the little girl was staying with an aunt."

"It says here," she said, motioning to the file, "that the general wanted you for insubordination, but your second lieutenant fought for you."

"He did," Archer said. "And he won that particular fight, but it didn't change the fact that the injuries I received took me out of active service."

Her eyebrows furrowed and then released before she set her warm stare on him. "When I asked you why you left the military, why didn't you tell me this story? Why did you simply say your body couldn't handle it?"

"Would it have mattered?" he asked honestly.

She held his gaze. "It's the truth, and it's a good truth. You saved a little girl when you'd been ordered not to." She fell silent then, watching him closely.

He felt any barrier between them begin to fall. He waited for her to say something more, but when she didn't, he asked, "Why do you think Penny wanted you to see this?"

She gave a soft smile, so foreign for her. "Probably to show me you're a good guy."

He became trapped in her gaze, free of all her usual guards. "Is that what you think of me? That I'm a good guy."

"In my line of work, I have a really hard time thinking anyone is good, but..." She held his gaze for so long that he thought she wasn't going to answer. Then she surprised him. "You're more than a good man, Archer. You're...incredible." And with that loaded statement hanging in the air between them, she rose and dropped her towel, revealing her gorgeous body, rosy nipples taut.

"Christ, you're warm," he told her, sliding his hands across her back to her bottom, where he squeezed. "So soft."

She took his face in her hands, stared at him intimately, and kissed him thoroughly, her tongue pulling the heat from deep in his gut, and then she met him with half-lidded eyes. "You're not soft at all."

"No, I'm not. What are you going to do about that?"

He saw it then, the shift in her. When she realized he needed her. The warmth of her. The reminder that those cold memories of death and bloodshed were in the past. She reached for his T-shirt, removing it in a hurry, then she headed for her drawer next to the bed. He made quick work to rid himself of his remaining clothing. He followed her every move as she took out a condom, feeling happy to be there in the present, yet a shadow of himself remained back in the past. Both parts needed her.

He wondered if she knew that as she sheathed him with the condom, then straddled him. He thrust his hands into her hair while she lifted up and took him all the way in. One easy stroke.

But then there was nothing easy about the way she took him. She rode him hard, rough, passionately forcing the chill to leave and only the warmth of her to remain in its wake. His rough breathing followed hers, no space between them. He didn't try to kiss her, and she didn't try either; he simply stared into her steady, heated gaze, letting her pull him back from the dark place his mind had gone.

She brought them both to orgasm swiftly and urgently, leaving him bucking and jerking his release while she crashed over the edge, shuddering her pleasure, drawing out his. Until the chill was replaced with something sweeter, far more tender.

"You know what I truly think?" she said many minutes later, her forehead resting against his.

"What's that?" he asked, sliding his hands up and down her back.

She leaned back, and he caught tears in her eyes. "That little girl was very lucky you were there to save her." He was still deep inside her, and she made no move to shift off him. "I wish back when I was little, you'd been there to save me too."

Emotion choking up his throat, he gathered her in his arms, holding her tight, doing what he could do for her now. "I wish I was there, too."

11

"*Hide, baby girl,*" *Mom gasped, shoving Elise under the bed. "Hide and don't come out. No matter what happens. Promise me?"*

"Mommy, I'm scared," Elise cried, clinging to her mother's shirt.

"I know, baby, but you're going to be all right. Promise me you won't come out?"

"I promise."

"Good girl." Mom kissed one cheek and then the other and forcibly shoved her. "Go. Go now. As far into the corner as you can go."

Elise slid back on her hip against the hardwood floor until she was pressed against the wall, tucking her legs in tight. Mom's feet ran by, and Elise heard the window open seconds before the bedroom door slammed open.

"You don't run, bitch," Dad roared. "You never run from me." Mom cried out in pain when Dad got close. "Where is Elise? Where did you put her?"

"She's gone," Mom yelled. "I put her out the window and told her to run. You'll never get her."

"You'll never get her either," Dad snarled.

Elise shut her eyes, covering her ears, bracing herself for the yelling to start. The screaming always came next. His fists followed.

But those familiar sounds never came. Other sounds did, soul-crushing sounds. Until...there were no sounds at all.

Elise jolted awake, sitting up with a gasp, clinging at her chest against the memory flooding her. "Jesus," she breathed, forcing herself to remember she wasn't that little girl anymore. She wasn't afraid. She wasn't weak. She wasn't out of control any longer.

"Nightmare?"

She started at the low voice and the warmth at her back. Until she remembered how she and Archer had talked late into the night and then she fell asleep, wrapped in his arms. He'd told her all about being raised by a single mom after his dad died tragically in war, his good childhood and his military life, and she told him all about her life with her aunt and uncle and everything she'd never told anyone but Zoey, Hazel, and Penny. They'd talked about their teenage years, the first kisses, their first times. All of it had seemed so natural last night. With Archer, it was warm and safe. She felt safe, something she'd really never felt before.

Suddenly, he sat up, sliding a comforting hand on her bare thigh, his brow wrinkling. "You okay?"

She nodded and laid back, breathless, catching sight of a sleepy Archer. He was many things. Strong, seductive, but this side of him, this sweet, almost boyish side was her favorite. "Yeah, I'm okay." She ran her hands over her face, suddenly aware she was shaking. "It's not a nightmare."

"Sure looked like a nightmare."

She dropped her hands and flipped onto her side to face him. "Sometimes I dream about the day my mom was murdered."

He gave her a pained look and lay back down beside her. "That's what this was? A memory of that day?"

She nodded. "It's...jarring."

He rested his head on his hand, sliding the other one along her exposed thigh beneath her nightgown. "No doubt it would be."

She liked that touch on her leg, the comfort it gave. More than that, she liked how his expression didn't drown in pity.

His steely gaze bore into hers, the boyish charm gone, only a resounding strength there now. "Are you seeing the dream from your eyes?"

She shook her head. "No, it's like I'm an outsider, almost like a movie."

He stroked his fingers across her skin, seeping warmth into her thigh. "And you see the whole thing?"

"I only see the part where my mom locked us in her bedroom. She shoved me under the bed and told me to hide. Then opened a window."

"Why'd she do that?"

"To protect me." Elise took a deep breath to settle the racing of her heart and to stuff back the rising emotions the memory always brought. "She told my father she'd helped me out the window and that I ran to get help."

Archer's brows drew together, thoughtful. "Amazingly brave of her to do that."

"Very brave," Elise agreed. "She must have been absolutely terrified, but I have no doubt she never would have expected he'd take her life and then his own."

"Is that part in your dream?"

She swallowed. Hard. Then forced the words out, wanting him to know this about her. "Just the gunshots and the thuds of their bodies hitting the ground."

"Jesus, Elise," Archer said, pulling her closer, like he

thought that would protect her. "That never should have happened to you."

"It never should have happened to my mom either, but love screws people's heads up."

"Not a good kind of love."

At that, Elise hesitated. "What is that? A good kind of love?"

"The love Rhys and Zoey have," he said without hesitation. "The love I've seen with my mother and her new husband. Healthy love."

"Have you ever had that?"

"No, but I also wasn't in a situation to go all in with someone during the military. I saw how hard my mother had it as a single mom. I wouldn't have done the same to my wife and possible children."

But I'm not in the military anymore, seeped into the air between them.

Silence descended swiftly, and it didn't feel entirely comfortable. It felt like there were things unsaid between them. To fill the silence, Elise blurted out, "I guess we fell asleep last night, huh?"

He chuckled, low and throaty. "You do have a way of exhausting me."

"Considering I blacked out too, I'd say the same back to you." She laughed and then noticed the clock on her nightstand. It read 7:16 AM. Well aware of the busy day ahead of her, she slid out of bed. "We better get up and moving." But she stopped short when her cell phone rang next to her clock. She grabbed it and smiled. "You're up early," she said, putting Penny on speaker.

"I don't even want to talk about it," her friend grumbled.

"You're on speaker," Elise added quickly. "Archer is here."

"Morning," Archer said.

"Morning." Penny's loud yawn crackled through the

phone line. "I thought you'd like to know that the cops have solved your break-in case. Give them a while, and I'll bet they'll call to update you."

"Was it related to the Phoenix case?" Elise asked.

"Nope," Penny said. "It was about your Wadsworth case."

Elise blinked. And blinked again. "Calvin Wadsworth broke into my office?" She heard the disbelief in her own voice.

Penny laughed. "Well, no, not him. He hired a thief-for-hire."

Elise slowly shook her head. Sure, she hadn't known for sure Connie or Isaac were involved in the break-in, but she certainly didn't expect Mr. Wadsworth to be behind the crime. "I need you to explain all this to me."

"Okay, I'll give you the short version from what I'm seeing on the report," Penny said. "Calvin found out his wife hired you to find evidence of his cheating. Maybe his wife was pissed and told him. Who knows. Anyways, I guess he's been planning to divorce Mrs. Wadsworth, and the prenup she signed would basically give her half of his money if he cheated. Obviously, he needed to get your evidence. Hence, the break-in."

Even Archer was shaking his head. "How did the police find out Wadsworth was behind it?"

"The fingerprints they found matched a kid already in the database," Penny reported. "They brought him in, and to get a lighter sentence, he gave up Wadsworth. The old man came in and confessed it all."

"Damn," Elise said.

"Right," Penny agreed. "Anyways, that's all I've got for now. Good luck this morning. Toodles."

The phone line went dead.

"Well, we've got our answer for that, then," Elise said.

"We do." Archer gave his head another hard shake. "People are truly unbelievable."

"You have no idea," Elise said, heading for her closet, waiting...and waiting...

"What did Penny mean by 'good luck this morning'?"

Elise smiled to herself. Of course, he wouldn't miss that. "I'm going to meet with Isaac."

A pause. Then Archer's voice hardened to a tone she'd never heard from him before. "Say that again?"

Yeah, she'd expected his displeasure on this particular subject. A month ago, she would've thrown some witty remark his way and steamrolled over his dominance. Now she knew him and where his protective side came from—a good place. She ditched her nightgown and took out a pair of panties and a cotton bra, sliding into them. "You're not going to be difficult about this, are you?" she called.

The heavy silence continued until she exited the closet in her lingerie. Archer sat up in bed, looking like a woman's dream come true with a body earned from hard work and dedication. "When I asked you to help on this case, I never requested you directly speak to the people involved."

Late last night, she'd caught him up on everything Penny discovered about Connie and Isaac. He wasn't pleased then, considering things only seemed to be getting more confusing and more twisted, and he certainly didn't sound it now. She chose a pencil skirt from her closet, and as she slid into it, she asked, "Did you forget this is my job?" She took a pink silk blouse and white camisole off the hanger and slipped into it. "I need to get into his head, and to do so, I need to meet him."

Archer frowned from the bed. "Where exactly is this meeting going to happen?"

"At a restaurant in midtown at 10 AM." His frown deepened, so she added, "I'm a possible investor in his new startup."

His tough demeanor broke for a moment. Surprise glinting in his eyes. "Penny arranged that?"

"She did," Elise confirmed, tucking the blouse into her skirt. "Luckily for us, Penny slid me into his morning schedule." She did a little spin, holding out her arms when she stopped. "Well, once I get my hair and makeup done, do I look the part of a rich investor?"

His head cocked and eyes narrowed slightly in the seconds before he slid out of bed wearing only his boxer briefs. Dear God, Archer was not a *pretty* man; he was built from rough strength and hard angles. And it made keeping her clothes on difficult. "I don't like this," he said, reaching her in a few powerful strides. "Confronting people is my job. Your job is to hide in the shadows."

"My job is to trap the guilty," she countered. "That's exactly what I'm going to do."

He tipped his head back, his Adam's apple dipped. "We're a team, Elise." He cupped her face. "Always a team. That's how this works."

He took a pained breath, and she regretted not going about this in a way that fully included him. "You're right," she finally hedged. "We are a team in this, and I'm sorry. I'm not used to that. Usually, it's just me and Penny. How about we do this? Meet me at the restaurant. I've asked Penny to get me a table by the window so she can tape our meeting. You can watch from a distance."

His mouth met hers in the next second, and he kissed her like he meant it. Hard. With tongue. Only when he had her wiggling against him did he break the kiss, and he was smiling. "A much better—smarter—plan."

"Because it includes you?" she asked.

He grinned. "Exactly."

~

ARCHER STILL DIDN'T LOVE Elise's idea, even a couple of hours later. Sitting behind the wheel of his truck, he watched her from a distance on what looked like a date with a good-looking, rich man. He'd rather undergo a root canal. Penny had set Elise up in one of Manhattan's most expensive restaurants, a place Isaac likely visited often to discuss business outside of his office. From the outside, the restaurant didn't look like much. Only three tall windows faced the street, but they revealed a room full of happy customers. The brown brick on the exterior was faded in a way that looked purposefully done, but the large crystal chandeliers seen through the windows spoke of elegance. While Archer watched every laugh and smile Elise threw Isaac's way over the course of their brunch meeting, his imagination began to run wild. He might have no claim on her...yet, but his heart hadn't gotten the memo. Gut twisting, he grabbed his wallet from the dash, pulled out Penny's card, and dialed her number. The ringing came through his truck's speakers.

She answered on the third ring. "I guess I shouldn't be surprised you're calling me," she said, voice amused.

He guessed he shouldn't have been either. "I've got no doubt you're already listening to their conversation. Get me ears too."

Penny laughed in a way that told Archer she'd read right through him. "Hot and smart. Oh, Elise is a lucky girl. Gimme a sec here." Archer had a moment to wonder if Elise had talked to Penny about him before she added, "Switching you over now."

A click followed by static filled the speakers of his truck before Elise's voice came through clearly. "I'm a new investor, as you know, but I've got old money I'd like to stretch a little."

Damn, she was a good liar. Archer made a mental note not to forget that.

Isaac sipped his Bloody Mary, then set it back onto the table. "We're always looking for new investors."

Elise studied him intently before leaning back in her seat. "I've heard good things about you from a friend in California."

"Who might that friend be?"

"Gwen Michaelson."

"Ah," Isaac drawled. "We have done some business together before."

Of course, Elise had likely researched all his ties before coming to this meeting. Archer liked watching her smart mind manipulate and outsmart her opponent. Especially when that smart mind of hers was aimed on someone who'd pissed him off.

Elise finished taking a sip of her mimosa before lowering her glass back to the table. "I do, however, have some concerns before we proceed."

"Which are?"

"Your brother."

Archer held his breath, waiting...watching. Isaac was obviously thrown off, if the straightening of his spine was any indication.

"My brother?" he asked, clearing his throat and shifting in his seat.

Elise didn't look rattled, her chin lifted, gaze narrowed on Isaac across the table. "I've been hearing you and he are having personal troubles that may affect anyone doing business with you. Is this true?"

"This is the first I'm hearing of it," Isaac said, the portrait of calm. "Can I ask what it is you've heard?"

"Rumblings about his wife."

At that, Isaac froze unnaturally. Archer saw it, and by the way Elise cocked her head, he knew she'd seen it too.

Again, Isaac cleared his throat. "I'm afraid, Ms. Norton"—the alias Elise had given him—"I have no idea what you're talking about. My brother and his wife are very happily married. In fact, did you know he's recently been nominated for the U.S. Attorney position?"

"No, I had not heard," Elise said before she folded her arms on the table, leaning in. "Let me make myself perfectly clear. I'm about making money. As long as I have your reassurance that whatever is going on in your personal life doesn't affect your business, I have no doubt we can make this work."

"There is no trouble in my personal life, of that I am certain," Isaac said firmly.

"Excellent," Elise said with a light voice, rising. She offered her hand. "Then I'll be in touch soon to discuss plans for our future."

Isaac returned the handshake. "I look forward to it."

Archer kept his focus on Isaac as Elise strode away. He waited for Isaac to pick up the phone, make a call, do something. All he did was pay the bill, leave through the front door, and wait only a short time until his driver drove up in a black Mercedes.

Before Archer could even move, the passenger side of his truck opened, and Elise jumped in, slamming the door behind her. "Go."

Archer didn't think twice. He hit the gas, moving into traffic. "Where are we going?"

"Follow Isaac, three cars up." She fastened her seat belt. "You heard all that, I presume?"

Damn, he was becoming predictable. "I did." He kept his attention on the Mercedes. "I take it you have a plan?"

"Just planted a seed," Elise said. "Now, let's see what he does with it."

Archer stayed a few cars back during the drive, but he sank back farther when they entered the Upper East Side. The Mercedes slowed, then came to a stop next to a row of fancy town houses lining the street. The massive, four-story homes were steps away from Central Park, and the building's façade was limestone with wrought-iron gates around each porch.

When Isaac got out and began climbing the porch steps, Archer pulled into a parking spot a few cars back.

Next to him, Elise stayed silent and alert, ready.

Until she said, "Well, shit, that's not who I was expecting him to go to."

Archer understood as the front door opened. The person on the porch was Connie, wearing a white T-shirt and jogging pants, with her hair up in a ponytail. They talked for a minute and then Isaac went into the house, and the door shut behind him. "I'm trying to wrap my head around this," Archer admitted. "Every time I've seen Connie at the club or at a fundraiser and such, she is dressed to the nines with a full face of makeup. Seeing her so casual tells me she's obviously staying here."

"Yeah, she obviously is." Elise reached for her phone and began snapping pics. "And this isn't the house she shares with her husband." She hit a few buttons on her phone.

The phone line rang once. "Whatcha got for me?" Penny asked.

"We're currently looking at Isaac and Connie, but I've got no clue whose house we're at. Can you check?"

"Yeah, okay, one sec…" The clicking of Penny's fingers hitting her keyboard filled the phone line. "It's a rental property," she eventually said. "Rented by Isaac's company."

Elise slowly shook her head like she was having as hard of

a time processing this as Archer was. "Okay, let me get this straight," Elise finally said. "Connie is staying in a rental property owned by her husband's brother, even though she and her husband are still happily married?"

"Even weirder," Penny drawled. "I learned a little bit ago that she and her husband are going to a fundraiser together tonight."

"None of this makes any sense," Archer grumbled. "What the fuck are these two up to?"

Elise slowly shook her head. "We need to figure out what that is and hear what they're saying. How do we make that happen?"

"We bug them," Archer said.

"Agreed," Penny said, then paused. "I know someone who can handle that for us, but they're not cheap."

"I actually know someone who's very cheap," Archer said. He grinned at Elise. "This is in my wheelhouse."

"Sounds good to me," Penny said, even though Elise seemed to have reservations. "I'll get the tech ready."

"That works," Archer said. "You'll be in touch when we're good to go?"

"You know it," Penny replied.

The phone line went dead.

Archer smiled at the pursing of Elise's lips. "You don't think I'm capable of installing a bug?" The thought was almost laughable, but he realized Elise didn't know the soldier. She only knew Phoenix's Head of Security.

"I've got no doubt you're capable," she said, eyes searching his. "It's just…risky."

Now, this, he liked. A lot, in fact. He couldn't hold back his smile and leaned in, cupping her chin. "Are you worried about me, Elise?"

She blushed, something she didn't do often. "We just don't know what we're up against or why this is happening. I don't like sending anyone into that situation. You're going in blind."

"Ah, I see." He brushed his thumb across her bottom lip, wishing they could forget Connie's and Isaac's bullshit all together and get lost in each other. "You know what I think?"

"What's that?" she asked, her voice husky.

"That you *are* worried about me. And I like it." Things were shifting between them, and he liked where that shift was taking them. He closed the distance and pressed his mouth against hers, relishing in the way her lips parted, inviting him in to take anything he wanted. "Keep doing that, all right?"

When she backed away, she rolled her eyes. "Again, don't go getting a big head about it."

"Oh, I'm getting a big *something* about it." He winked, and her infectious laughter filled the truck as he drove away.

12

*E*lise had spent the remainder of the day sitting behind her desk, keeping an eye on Connie and Isaac through the location on their cell phones. *Thank you, Penny.* Both stayed at the house for a couple of hours but parted ways after. Connie went home to her husband. Isaac went back to work. Elise dug harder, looking through all the files Penny sent her way. Even after hours of searching, she hit a dead end. They hadn't taken another step out of place. No one approached Rhys to blackmail him over sharing more details about Phoenix. But an idea began to present itself right as her cell phone rang. One look at the screen revealed it was Archer.

She hit the speakerphone. "I was just about to call you," she said by way of greeting.

"I beat you to it, then."

She smiled at the warmth in his voice. "Can I go first, or do you have something pressing to tell me?"

"Go ahead. My news can wait."

Elise turned in her swivel chair, staring out at the city skyline, the sun nearly blinding against one of the windows of the skyscraper. "The police called to tell me they made an arrest on my break-in. Both the professional thief and Mr. Wadsworth."

"Good news," Archer said.

"Yeah." She paused, sensing a question lingering in the air between them: *will you still stay tonight?* A question she didn't feel needed answered. She already knew he would want to, and she'd want that too. "The other thing I've been sitting here thinking about is, do you think this is a kink for Connie and Isaac?"

"A kink?"

"They like to watch, right? Maybe they get off on being watched too? And for them, exposing the photograph is their kink. To see themselves in the media, exposed for all to see, got them off? It's like playing out a fantasy but with no real risk, because their identities weren't exposed."

"It's possible," he said. "Of course, it would terminate their membership, but it's a lot less of a headache for us."

"It is," she said. "But it's just one theory because I can't think of anything else, and there are so many loose ends that we need to keep on this until we know for sure."

"Agreed," he said. "Which brings me to my news. Penny texted. We're all set to go after sundown."

"Excellent. Where are we meeting?"

A pause. "Why don't you come up to my place tonight? A change of scenery might be nice."

She smiled. She kept waiting for that spike of panic to creep up since she was letting things happen with Archer she never let happen, but it simply never came. She wasn't sure where this was going between them, but she didn't want to stop it either. "Sounds good. What time?"

"Whenever you're done," he said. "I'm home now. I'm sending you my address. See you soon."

Her phone dinged, and the text message crossed the

screen. "Bye." She ended the call, then sent Hazel a quick text. Cops called today. They made an arrest on the break-in. You're all safe. Nothing to worry about. Won't be home tonight. Staying at Archer's.

Elise powered off her computer and scooped out her purse from her drawer when Hazel's reply dinged on her phone: Just friends, huh?

Elise replied with the tongue-sticking-out emoji and left it at that. Even she couldn't explain exactly what was going on or where they were headed, so she decided to just let what was happening, happen and felt good. She felt safe, felt...*happy*. She made it outside quickly after locking up her office and gave Keith a wave on her way out the door before hailing a cab. Twenty minutes later, she was surprised to find Archer lived in the pricey East Village neighborhood, not far from Union Square. Apparently, Rhys paid him well if he could afford this place. She reached security and was quickly approved to enter. When she stepped into the elevator, she found buttons that led to a rooftop pool, fitness center, and courtyard garden. She hit floor six, and the elevator whizzed up. When it opened, she found Archer leaning against the door with a smile on his face.

"Hey," he said, wearing all black and looking damn fine in it.

She returned the smile. "Hey."

"Come." He gestured down the hallway. "I've got a surprise for you."

She followed him to the third apartment door down on the right. When she entered, she found a sleek, contemporary space with floor-to-ceiling windows showing off the city she loved. The adjoining kitchen was clean, with white lines and stone countertops. But all that took a back seat to the roast beef dinner set out on the kitchen table near the windows. "What's all this about?"

He slid in behind her, wrapping his arms around her. "I cooked for you."

"You did?" She spun around, lacing her hands behind his neck, again waiting for the unease to spiral through her. *A date.* This was a date, and she didn't hate it. All the heat and tension that had once been there had shifted into something much more...real. "That was very nice of you. It smells delicious." She gave him a quick kiss, which she ended before it could go any further, then took the seat he pulled out for her.

He poured two glasses of wine, then joined her and dug in.

She ate a bite of the beef and nearly purred in happiness. "I had no idea you can cook."

"I can grill a mean steak," he said with a soft smile. "But this recipe, my mom taught me as a kid, and truly, you can't screw it up."

"I probably could," she said. "Cooking isn't really my forte; that's why Hazel always cooks for me."

"She's a good friend, Hazel?" he asked, cutting into his dinner.

"The best. Her, Zoey, and Penny," Elise said before taking a sip of her wine. "We're just very, very close. Like sisters. Do you have anyone like that?"

"Rhys, Hunt, and Kieran," he said between bites. "It's just like that."

"What about before them?"

He finished chewing before he answered, "Not like what you have with Hazel. I've lived a handful of lives, and within those lives, I've had different groups of friends. My longest friendship is with Rhys. I've known him since before my first deployment, and we met Hunt and Kieran when I was back on leave the first time."

She studied him, peeling back all his layers. When he'd suggested installing the bug himself, she was shocked. Until she remembered he was a retired Green Beret. Being a shadow, getting in and out, and placing a bug was likely something he'd considered easy in his military life.

A soft laugh drew her from her thoughts. Archer's brows lifted. "Why are you looking at me like a puzzle you can't quite figure out?"

She laughed as well, shrugging. "I guess I'm wondering who you truly are."

He wiped his mouth with his napkin. "Who I am?"

"Yeah."

His look turned measured. "I've been a pretty open book, don't you think?"

"Sort of," she said, the confusing thought suddenly becoming clear. "But as you said, you've lived a lot of lives. Your life with your mom. Your life with the military. Your life with Rhys and the guys. Are you happy with *this* life you have now?"

"Very happy."

She looked for any hint of a lie on his face and didn't find any. "You're content, then, with running security for Phoenix, simply heading up teams that handle all the action?"

"Extremely content. I enjoy my job, and I know at the end of it, I might not die."

She pushed the mashed potatoes around on her plate and smiled. "Okay, I guess that's a plus. But don't you miss all the excitement, the adventure?"

He shook his head. "I don't look to the past, only to the future."

"And this life, the one you're living, makes you happy?"

His silence was his reply. She thought he wasn't going to answer, but then he surprised her. He lifted his intense stare to her. "Right now, at this very moment, I am the happiest I've been, maybe ever."

She couldn't look away from him, not when his soul was bared. She instinctively replied. "Me too."

Their gazes held for a long moment, her insides quivering, the intensity rich on the air.

Until her cell phone beeped, breaking the stare. She started and jerked her focus to the screen revealing a text from Penny: GOT THE BLUEPRINTS. REVIEW THEM WITH BOY TOY. Elise read the text aloud.

"Let me have a look." He wiped his hands, then accepted the phone, and Elise could barely take her eyes off him.

She'd seen Archer be irritating, sensual, and sweet, but this side, the lethal soldier, nearly made her bones melt as he took his time studying where he was going, forming a plan. "All right. Simple enough." He returned her phone and focused back on his dinner.

The rest of the meal was eaten in comfortable silence. They quickly cleaned up, and he discussed his plan for getting in and out fast. "I've got something for you," she said, taking an ear communicator out of her purse and offering it to him. "You're not going in there alone."

"I wouldn't have expected otherwise." He grinned.

She found herself moving closer, pulled by the warmth he offered and the strength he possessed. "I would tell this to anyone else I'm working with, so I'll say it to you: Don't be an idiot. We're not superheroes. No one gets hurt under my watch. Ever. We investigate, not fight. Any presence of danger, you get out. Got it?"

His grin widened. "Yes, ma'am."

"What's that smile about?" she asked, wiggling into him.

He dipped his chin, bringing his mouth within an inch of hers. "I was just thinking there was a time I got really irritated when you got bossy."

She lifted her brows at him. "And now?"

He had her by the waist and yanked her against him.

Tight. Until all she could feel were the hard lines of his body. "I'm growing rather fond of you telling me what to do." He sealed his mouth over hers, devouring her laughter. He kissed her roughly, passionately with his tongue dancing with hers until she had this deep, foreign need not let him go and to keep him safe.

When he broke the kiss, breathless, she reopened her eyes. "Promise me you'll be safe."

He gave her another kiss. A soft one. One that felt different than any other kiss before it. "I promise."

THE TOWN HOUSE lay dark and quiet as Archer, dressed in black cargo pants and a black long-sleeve T-shirt and beanie hat, made his way to the back door through the garden. It'd been a long time since he ran a mission, but he'd run many just like this. His instincts sharpened, everything become alert, and his surroundings becoming clear.

"I've disabled the security system," Penny said through his ear communicator. "You've got ten minutes tops to get in and out before they figure out the system is down."

Archer didn't respond; Penny already knew he wouldn't. The sound of a voice carried even when someone thought it didn't. Getting the okay to enter, he used his thin screwdriver to unlock the deadbolt and then the lock on the door handle. The bugs were in his pocket, and once he was inside, he kept his focus on getting them in place and getting out. He went to the most challenging spot first. From what he knew of people, most conversations happened in three places, no matter who you were or where you lived. The bedroom, living room, and the kitchen. From the blueprints Penny had given him earlier, he knew the master bedroom was on the third floor.

Once he entered the house, he quickly noted the silence, the darkness. The town house had three levels, with an unfinished basement below. Following the image in his mind, he headed up the stairs, keeping his small flashlight turned off until he reached the master bedroom. He hurried to the nightstand and used the light to guide his way to attach the bug to the backside of the stand, low to the ground, where no one would find it.

"First bug is activated," Penny said through the ear communicator.

Clicking off the thin flashlight, he moved swiftly back downstairs and installed the next bug in the living room, beneath the television stand.

"Second bug up," Penny acknowledged.

Right as Archer went to move toward the kitchen, he spotted movement in front of the living room window.

He ducked behind the main wall separating the hallway from the living room, holding his breath as Elise said, "Shit. Isaac is on the porch. He's coming inside."

"Alarm reactivated," Penny said.

The fear in Elise's voice rattled Archer for a moment. Not only was he not used to his team being scared, but he also wasn't used to Elise being scared of anything. It touched on an unknown place in his heart. But this, he did know how to handle. He blended into the shadows, staying perfectly still.

The front door opened and shut, and the hall light flicked on. Isaac hit the button to rearm the alarm. His shoes clicked against the floor as he strode by and headed up the stairs quickly, indicating he didn't plan to stay long. Neither did Archer.

When all was clear and Archer heard Isaac walk into the bedroom upstairs, he silently hurried down the hallway to the kitchen. There, he attached the bug to the bottom of the fridge, working in pure darkness.

"Third bug activated," Penny said. "Boy, you got balls."

Archer embraced the energy flowing through his veins. At one time in his life, he'd lived for this, the adrenaline, the danger. He did miss the action, and it felt good to stretch his mind this way again. He stayed silent, waiting for Penny's order.

It came a second later. "The back door has been deactivated from the alarm."

Archer didn't wait, he slowly opened the door he came in through, waiting for the single beep to indicate the alarm had detected the door was opened, but it never came. *Good work, Penny.* Using his tools, he relocked the door behind him before blending back into the shadows. He kept pressed against the brick wall, waiting to ensure no kitchen lights came on and Isaac hadn't heard him leave.

A minute later, Elise said over the communicator, "Isaac has just left again through the front door."

Archer took that as an all clear for him to move. He jogged out of the garden and climbed the tall fence. He landed hard on the other side, then quickly removed the black beanie covering his hair and jogged down one street and then another, until he came to the meeting spot with Elise: a small park a few blocks away. She was in the darkest corner of the lawn, away from the busy street, pacing near a mature shade tree.

He couldn't help but smile. "Worrying about me looks good you."

She gasped and spun around, eyes fraught with concern before she threw herself at him. "Holy shit, that was close." She gripped his shirt like she'd never let him go. "Why didn't you say you were out?"

"It's not safe to ever talk," he said, breathless from the run. "Besides, I got back here fast enough."

"Jesus, that was close." She bounced on her feet. "Hell, I like investigating, but this shit, tonight, that's over my head."

Not minding her concern, he slid a hand low on her back, reveling in the adrenaline ripping through his veins. "Nah, it wasn't that close."

"Are you kidding?" she gasped. "Isaac came into the house."

"He went right upstairs," Archer said, blowing out a long breath to settle the race of his heart as sweat ran down his spine. "Had no idea I was there, which is exactly the point."

She shook her head, her skin slightly pale. "I thought you were totally going to get caught."

"Never," he said, leaning in and giving her a playful grin. "You keep forgetting my past. I was in absolutely no danger tonight." He paused to wink. "Sometime, I'll tell you about the really dangerous missions, and then you'll have good reason to look so pale."

"I think I might pass on that," she said, breathing out a long, slow breath. "Shit, Archer." Her hand came to her heart like she was containing it from beating right out of her chest, her pretty, wide eyes searching his.

And slowly, as the seconds drew on, a truth became clear —they were falling for each other. Maybe she knew it too, maybe she didn't, but he felt the shift between them. But he saw another truth too—caring for someone was hard for her. He saw it all over her face now, clear as day, and he knew why. Her father had caused this. She didn't let many people in. She had her close-knit group of friends. Now Archer was a part of that, and he saw the fear rippling on her expression. It wasn't just that he'd been in danger; it was that she cared enough that it scared her he might get hurt. Because that's what had happened in her life. She'd lost people tragically.

"I'm right here, Elise," he murmured. "Safe."

Their gazes held for a beat before something broke.

Something frantic and needy and desperate to get as close as possible so nothing could ever come between them. His mouth met hers, and she kissed him like she needed him to breathe, and he returned the intensity tenfold.

She ripped at his belt, her fingers rushing to expose him. "Condom," she gasped.

He quickly had his wallet out and a condom in his hand before dropping his wallet onto the ground. While he sheathed himself, she got one leg out of her pants, with her panties pulled to the side. He didn't hesitate; he pinned her to the tree behind them, lifted her leg, and drove into her. Her unforgettable moans brushing by his ear.

Frantic moans. Desperate moans.

He wasn't sweet in his movements, and this wasn't love-making. It was something else entirely. Something raw and real, and he thrust deeper, desperate to fill all of her with all of him. Urgent for her to feel she would never be alone and scared ever again, and that he needed her all the same. This was need and acceptance all in one. His touch was rough, and she gripped his arms painfully tight, for all the same reasons he ground himself into her, leaving no space between them.

He shifted up hard into her, unable to get as close as he wanted. To keep her safe like she wanted to keep him safe. Faster and faster and harder and deeper, he gave all of himself to her until her breath hitched and she began convulsing with her release. He rode her harder, letting her climax draw his out. Until all the pressure deep in his groin erupted, pulsating his semen into the condom, yanking deep groans from his chest.

Until all that remained was their heavy breathing, the traffic off in the distance, and the awareness that nothing lay between them anymore but open hearts and open minds.

He had no intention of withdrawing from her sweet heat

massaging him with the lingering effects of her orgasm, nowhere near done with her. Until Penny quipped through the earbud, "Listen, I know you guys are kinky, but how about we save that shit for when you're not wearing an ear com."

Archer burst out laughing. "Sorry, Penny." He ripped the earbud from his ear, disabling communication.

"Dammit," Elise said with a laugh, panting, her head back against the tree, eyes closed tight. "I'm going to owe her so big for that one."

He chuckled, brushing her hair away from her sweaty face. "Totally worth it, though."

She slowly opened her satiated eyes, and her soft laugh eased a whole lot of weight in his chest as she said, "Totally worth it."

13

A month had gone by in a whirl of spectacular sex and...*happiness.* Elise had worked five cases during the past four weeks, and she and Archer had fallen into a groove she didn't want to fall out of. There wasn't a night they weren't together, even if it was only sleeping together because Archer got home late from working at the club. Hell, they were more of a couple than she'd ever "coupled" with anyone. But with all the good, also came the frustration that she had yet to close the investigation on Connie and Isaac. She had listened to every one of their conversations, recorded from the bugs, every day, for the last month...and nothing. Her theory about this being their kink was beginning to seem likely, but something in Elise told her to keep pressing forward. So she did what she always did when things got tense; she spent the morning jogging along the East River to clear her head. But even after a hot shower, she felt stalled on the next steps. There was only one thing she hated more than not closing a case. Not closing *Archer's* case. Especially when Rhys sent a text asking her to stop by their house this morning for an update. So, just after nine o'clock in the morning, Elise made her way into Manhattan.

When she reached Rhys and Zoey's apartment, her cell phone rang in her purse. A quick look at the screen revealed her aunt and uncle were calling. "Good morning," she said after she answered the FaceTime.

"Hi, sweetie," her aunt Marylin said, and Uncle Joe waved his greeting.

Aunt Marylin had warm bright-blue eyes, mid-length blonde hair that was sun kissed by the Florida sun. Uncle Joe was fit from his long career with the New York City Police Department. His gray hair had thinned in recent years, but his mischievous smile remained unchanged. "You two are so tan."

"You can't avoid the sun here," Aunt Marylin said. "How are things at home?"

"Same," Elise answered. They'd become snowbirds after they retired, and loved Florida so much they never returned to New York City. Zoey, Hazel, and Penny had filled the void of the missing family. Horns honked, and a man crossing the street cursed out a driver who nearly hit him. Elise laughed. "New York City is always the same."

"We definitely don't miss the hustle and bustle," Uncle Joe said. "How's work?"

"Busy. Which is good business."

Uncle Joe smiled. "Glad to hear it."

Aunt Marylin leaned in closer to her cell phone, examining her like only a caring mother would. "You look good."

Yeah, multiple orgasms for an entire month could do incredible things to the body. "I feel good."

Aunt Marylin gave a sly smile. "Is there a love interest we should know about that's causing you to look so happy?"

"Can't I look this happy just on my own?"

"Of course," Aunt Marylin countered. "But you've got a

certain sparkle in your eye. One that sure looks like a woman getting loved right."

Elise laughed softly. "Well, there might be someone."

"Oh?" Aunt Marylin quipped.

"It's new, but it's good," Elise cut in before she could get any ideas. The first good relationship she'd ever had with a man. One that she didn't wholly control, simply because Archer wasn't the type of man anyone controlled unless he allowed it.

"What's he do?" Uncle Joe asked.

"Head of Security for Rhys Harrington," she said, choosing her words carefully. Everyone in New York City knew the powerful Harrington name.

"Ah," Uncle Joe said. "In a similar field, then?"

Elise shrugged. "Sort of. He protects people. I catch the bad people."

"And you're damn good at it." Uncle Joe beamed with pride.

"Thanks." A beep followed by a message from Zoey asking when she would arrive popped up on her screen. "I'm sorry, but I've got to get to a meeting."

"We won't keep you," Aunt Marilyn said. "Love you lots, honey. We'll talk soon."

"Love you too." Elise waited for the typical waves goodbye before she ended the call. She would never forget what they had done for her, stepping in when Elise had no one. One day, she'd find a way to repay them. She quickly shoved her phone in her purse and entered Rhys' building.

Once she cleared security, she was in the elevator and on her way up to their apartment. A fancy place that looked beyond her means even if she worked her whole life. A quick knock on the door at the end of the hallway, and it opened to Rhys.

"Good morning," he said, stepping away from the door to allow her to enter.

"Mornin'." She followed him, kicking off her shoes at the door, scared to get dirt on anything. Zoey wouldn't have cared, but Rhys grew up and lived in another world. One with private schools, dinner parties, and people worth more money than Elise could ever dream up.

"Coffee?" he asked.

"Please."

He led her to the kitchen and quickly poured two cups. "Thanks for coming to see me this morning," he said, offering her a mug. "My day is full of off-site meetings, but I wanted to make sure we touched base."

She slid onto the stool at the counter and added sugar and cream to hers. "No problem. I know things aren't moving as quickly as you'd probably like."

"The club has been closed for a month now," he stated, stirring his coffee. "Members are growing restless, and we've already lost quite a few."

"I know it's frustrating," Elise said, feeling like she wasn't only letting Rhys down, but Archer too, since the breach landed on his shoulders. "But there's been zero activity. We've bugged the house Connie and Isaac visit. I'm following their paper trail, cyber trail, any trail, really. They're not taking a step sideways."

Rhys considered her, cocking his hand. "I want to reopen the club, but to do so, I need to revoke their memberships, which would mean confronting them. Is this a risk?"

"I think that's a hard question to answer," she admitted. "We don't know the real reason they sold the photo."

"What does your gut tell you?"

She appreciated how he trusted her, and she had the sense that Rhys only trusted her that much because Archer did.

"We need to wait. Something will come of this; there's a reason they did it."

"Then stay on them," Rhys said, without hesitation, running a hand over his face. "Everyone reveals themselves, eventually."

Elise nodded and then proceeded to go into a lengthy conversation about every single thing she'd discovered about Connie and Isaac. The good, the bad, and the boring. Until she reached the end of what she and Penny had learned. "And that's all I've got right now. Believe me, I'm equally as frustrated."

"I bet," Rhys said. "You're doing a good job for us. Keep me updated if anything more develops. We'll keep Phoenix closed for another couple weeks before we revisit the issue."

Elise accepted the order with a nod, taking a long sip of her coffee, one she nearly spit out as Rhys said, "On another front, I've been meaning to speak to you. I've had a request from a member that you partake in another show."

She set her coffee mug down. "Oh."

Rhys set that hard stare on her, assessing her. "Archer has offered to do the show with you, if you would like."

The offer was a direct hit to her heart, and she felt the coldness creep into all the spots Archer's touch had been healing this past month. "I told him I'm not interested in that."

Rhys' brows drew together tight, telling her, her raw emotions showed on her face. "I'm aware, but he also wanted to give you time to see if you had a change of opinion on that. He simply said that if you were interested in taking part in the show, he'd do the show with you."

Something deep and raw broke inside her, and that's when she knew, somewhere along the way, she'd let all her guards down. Even let herself believe he didn't need others to watch them to find fulfillment; he only needed *her*. She thought he saw her, liked her, and wanted her for what she was, not what he hoped she'd become—a woman who wanted to live his lifestyle.

"I asked him a while ago," Rhys said quickly, obviously reading something in her expression. "If things have changed and if I have overstepped, I'm sorry, Elise."

"No, it's fine," she said, sucking down that pain and placing it back into the spot in her chest where it'd stayed for years and locked it up tight. "Thank you for asking. Truly. But while I respect what you do for the members of your club, my time there was a one-shot deal."

"Understood," Rhys said with a soft smile, and yet his examination of her seemed even deeper now, like he read right through her. "Again, I'm sorry if I upset you."

"You didn't upset me," she countered, planting on a fake smile. "Everything is good."

A beat.

"What's wrong?" Zoey asked, entering the room and stopping dead.

Oh, God, she had to get out of there. She hurried off the stool. "Nothing is wrong. I just need to go." Feeling closed in, the walls squeezing her, she booked it to the front door.

The moment she got outside, into the hallway, Zoey called, "Elise. Wait."

Elise froze, shut her eyes, and breathed deep, feeling her throat tighten and her chin quiver.

"Talk to me. What's wrong?"

Zoey's soft voice didn't help any. Elise blew out the breath she'd been holding, then faced a worried Zoey. "I'm fine, really."

"Elise," Zoey said, taking Elise's hand. "Something is wrong. I can see it all over your face. The thing with friends is you can share. That's why we're here. What happened?"

Elise swallowed the emotion in her throat and only

addressed Zoey when she had her voice in check. "Rhys said a member wanted me to take part in a show."

Zoey frowned. "You do know he totally doesn't care if you say no."

"Yes, I know that." She hesitated and then realized Zoey was right—Elise did have friends. Three of the best. She didn't need to fight through life alone. "Archer said he'd do the show with me." She paused and huffed, shaking out her arms. "I don't even know why that bugs me. This is the life he lives. Of course, he'd want me to go back there with him."

"The life he *was* living," Zoey corrected.

Elise knew then and there a truth she'd been running from. "Then *why* wouldn't he tell his best friend, almost a brother, in the past month that things have changed between us and we've gotten more serious? That he didn't plan on partaking in the shows anymore?" Elise had told her friends. Right away. Without any hesitation.

Awareness rushed across Zoey's face. "Oh."

In the comfort of her good friend, her heart spilled free. "I asked him more than once if he needs the club to be happy, and he told me no. But clearly, that isn't true." All the safety she'd felt in the strength of his honest words smashed into pieces around her. "I need real, honest, and I'm just not sure this is that." Elise remembered the screaming, the gunshots, the blood. She remembered her mother staying even though it was the worst thing for her to do.

"Elise," Zoey said softly, taking her into a hug. "You deserve to be happy and to find real love, honest love." She leaned back to cup Elise's face. "You want that. You get that. No matter what."

Elise laughed softly, hating the tears in her eyes. "How about no love at all? That's easier." This was why she never crossed those damn emotional lines. Things weren't easy; they were complicated and messy. This edgy feeling, the fear coursing through her veins, this, she didn't want and was what she'd avoided at all cost. Why had she forgotten that?

"Nothing good is easy, my friend," Zoey said, wrapping Elise in the warmth of her embrace again. "Believe me, no matter how hard it is, love is worth it."

Elise returned the hug, knowing Zoey's advice was jaded. She had real love. True love. She'd never known broken love, not like Elise did. And she'd never end up like her mother. Unaware and desperate to make things work.

Not ever.

ARCHER STRODE out of his office in the late afternoon with an armful of files, each with a USB clipped to the front. He made his way to the end of the hallway and entered the meeting room already full of the staff he'd hired to run security at Phoenix. They all fell silent when he entered the room. The six-man team were all retired military, all wearing the Phoenix security attire of black T-shirts and black cargo pants.

"Thanks for coming in," Archer said to his team before he began handing out the file folders. "We've got two new members joining once we reopen the club: Carrie Henry and Eric Stewart." He took his spot at the front of the room, pressing his knuckles against the table. "Nothing stands out as troublesome, but as always, keep a close eye on them."

Around the table, heads nodded in agreement.

A long-time employee, Hawke skimmed through the file before he set his stern gray eyes on Archer. "I take it we have someone new handling the vetting?" Retired Navy SEAL, Hawke had lost a leg on a mission in Iraq, ending his military career. Within ten minutes of his interview, Archer had hired him, and they'd never looked back. Hawke had Archer's full trust.

Archer smiled, unsurprised Hawke didn't miss such a detail, and nodded. "We've got a new hacker in our ranks. She's good." After running the change by Rhys last month, Penny had gladly taken on the vetting process for new clients and now handled all intel for Archer, and Wayne had accepted being let go without a problem. Especially since, on Penny's advice, Archer had told Wayne that Penny was taking over. The kid had paled, indicating to Archer that Penny could make his life miserable if he caused trouble.

"She's...detailed," Hawke mused, flipping through the pages. He finally met Archer's gaze again. "Any word on the breach with the photograph?"

Frustration bit at Archer as he shook his head. "Looks like it was a one-off, but we're keeping a close eye on the situation." Ever since the news article came out, security had been on high alert.

Hawke nodded. "Good."

Archer scanned the table. "Any concerns?" The group stayed silent. Archer slapped the table. "Good. Let's keep doing what we're doing even when we're closed. Learn the new members. Watch their behavior from the videos on the USB files. Get acquainted with them." He said his goodbyes to his team before returning to his office.

Only his office was no longer empty. Rhys sat in the client chair.

The moment Archer entered the room, Rhys said grimly, "I think I fucked up."

Archer laughed softly, moving behind his desk and taking a seat. "That's not something you're usually so forthright about."

Rhys didn't laugh back. His intense stare bore into Archer. "Have things between you and Elise changed?"

The smile faded from Archer's face. "Why?"

"She came by the house this morning to update me on the case. I asked her if she wanted to take part in a show, and she looked incredibly hurt when I said you had agreed to do the show with her."

Archer's fingers curled.

Rhys lifted a brow. "So, I'll ask again, have things changed between you two?"

"They have," Archer admitted, only now realizing this was the first time he had admitted that aloud.

No accusation lay in Rhys' eyes, only concern. "Why hadn't you mentioned that?"

Archer hesitated. "I didn't feel the need. We haven't set anything in stone. We've just been letting things fall where they may."

"Well," Rhys stated with a frown. "They fell with her heart breaking in front of me this morning."

"Shit," Archer said.

"You got some mending to do." Rhys rose, moving to the door and then turned back. "She's hurt. Go fix that."

The thought rattled in Archer's head. He'd upset her, and he knew why. He'd given her a reason to doubt him. All her warranted fear and trust issues that had faded away had rebounded harder than ever.

Archer didn't wait around to fix this. He called; she ignored that. He texted her; she didn't respond. Desperate to correct his mistake, he hopped in a cab and went to her office. The security guard, Keith, who knew him well enough by now, let Archer breeze into the elevator, declaring that Elise was in her office. He found her sitting behind her desk. He didn't knock to give her the chance to shut him out; he opened the door. She lifted her head, and the hurt in her eyes nearly had him sinking to his knees. "You didn't answer my text or my call," he said, shutting the door behind him.

"Usually, that means a person wants to be left alone," she said, head bowed to her paperwork.

The ground felt unsteady beneath his feet as he approached her. "You're upset."

Her head lifted, as did her chin, and in a way so familiar to him, she said, "No, I'm not."

The shields in her eyes slammed up, forcing him out. "You don't look fine."

A beat passed.

Then came her long sigh before she hit him with the force of her stare. "You don't want me to do this."

"Do what?"

"Hear the emotional things about to come out of my mouth. I don't even want to say them. But that's where we are, and there is no changing that." She rose and headed for her door.

He stopped her by grabbing her arm. "Elise, talk to me."

She visibly swallowed, then met him with a gaze far away from there. "This isn't real, Archer."

"What isn't real?"

"Us. This. Whatever we've been doing here."

"It's real for me."

"Is it? Truly?" A coldness spread across him as she continued, "Because I remember when all this started, you said that you didn't want serious."

"I can't change my mind?"

The veil on her face fell, exposing the hurt. The pain he'd caused. "You never told Rhys about me, about us. About how things had changed. Not one single word about me to your friends?" Her voice blistered. "What am I? Your dirty little secret?"

"Absolutely not," he said, a tremble in his voice he'd never heard before.

"What about Hunt, Kieran? Have you told them?"

"Elise, it's not like—"

"I'll take that as you haven't told them." She drew in a long deep breath and blew it out slowly, shaking her head. "You're not fulfilled with me, and we've been lying to ourselves to think otherwise. This whole time, you were waiting for Phoenix to reopen, and you assumed I'd want to come with you, which I made perfectly clear I don't want."

Shit, he had no idea how to backpedal out of this conversation. Because he couldn't give her an answer for why he hadn't shouted to the world how amazing she was and how amazing they were together. Why the fuck hadn't he?

"It's all right, Archer, I'll let you off the hook," she said in his silence, and he saw any emotion she once had for him was gone. "We had fun. Lots of fun."

He saw the ending. He wanted to stop it. He parted his lips...

"But like we said from the very beginning, we had chemistry. We explored that. But neither of us was looking for anything serious." She smiled the fakest smile he'd ever seen in his life. "We're okay. Truly." She tried to hide the shake in her voice, but he heard it loud and clear. "Friends, all right?"

Friends. Fuck, friends.

"Elise," was the only damn thing he could say.

She tore her emotion-packed eyes off him and kissed his cheek. "I'll be in touch when, and if, the case develops further."

"Wait," he called.

She froze right as his cell phone beeped in his pocket.

"Fuck," he growled, reaching for his phone. Hawke texted: TROUBLE AT THE CLUB. GET HERE ASAP.

He responded: BE THERE IN 10.

Shoving his cell back into his pocket, he went to Elise, who had not moved, which only told him she wanted to know his thoughts. "Elise, look at me," he said to her back.

Slowly, she turned, and tears welled in her eyes. He cupped her face, holding her tight. "We're *not* just friends. Won't ever be just friends, and we both fucking know that. But I'm needed at the club."

"Then go," she said hoarsely.

"Can I come to you later so we can talk?"

She looked so damn tired. "What's the point? Where can this possibly go?"

His head felt foggy, and he didn't have the answers to fix this with her, so he did the only thing he could think to do. He grabbed her and kissed her with all the passion and emotion lacing his veins. When he broke the kiss, he added, "We'll talk later, all right?"

She nodded, but he saw in her eyes she was already distant.

They'd spiraled so deep he didn't even realize they'd gotten so lost in each other. He'd taken too much from her without offering her a safe place to land.

What he'd done wasn't right, and he hated himself for it.

---

14

*E*lise stared at the door Archer strode out of, feeling like her world was breaking apart, and she had no idea how to pull the pieces together again. She'd been happy, so damn happy with Archer. Why couldn't happiness last?

Minutes turned into an hour. Until she realized she wasn't alone in her office anymore. Zoey and Hazel rushed in, arms wrapping around Elise, and it was exactly what she needed right now. She sunk into their hold and did what she hadn't done for a very long time. She cried.

Only when her tears stopped flowing and she felt in control of her emotions did she lean away. "Thanks for coming all the way here," she said, wiping at her eyes. To Hazel, she added, "Thanks for worrying."

"You don't need to thank us for being good friends," Hazel said. "Of course, we'd be here."

Elise wiped another tear off her face. "How did you know I needed you?"

"Archer called a little bit ago," Zoey said. "He said he couldn't get away and thought you needed us."

How he could be so sweet and so clueless at the same

time only made Elise's head throb harder. "What happened at the club that was so urgent?"

"A reporter broke into one of the tunnels that led to the club. Archer and Hawke are dealing with her and the police, having her arrested for breaking and entering and clearing all that up."

Hazel cringed. "She works with me. My editor is all over the club story right now. She wants all the deets."

"She's not going to get any," Zoey said firmly. "Rhys and Archer are locking everything up super tight. And you'll never say a word."

"You're right about that," Hazel agreed, zipping up her lips. "Mum's the word." She gave Zoey her sweet smile, before that smile fell and she took a seat on Elise's desk. "Tell us what you're thinking."

Elise shrugged. "I don't even know what I'm thinking anymore. It's all just...messy."

Zoey gave a knowing look, taking a seat on the other side of the desk. "Most relationships are."

True, but this was even more complicated. "No matter how I look at this, it just can't work between us, so why pretend it could and let this go on any longer?"

"Why couldn't it work?" Hazel asked.

"Because I saw my father murder my mother, and I'm too afraid to open up unless it's safe. And Archer, by being one person with me and another with his friends, as well as lying to me about being okay with having a sex life away from the club, makes it not safe for me."

Zoey blinked.

Hazel blinked.

Greeted by their shocked expressions, Elise snorted a laugh. "What?"

"You've just never spoken so openly about your feelings like that," Zoey said, like Elise had horns growing out of her head.

"Ever," Hazel agreed with big eyes.

Elise hadn't really considered that, but she realized they were right. "Okay, so maybe Archer's gotten me out of my shell a little."

"A lot out of your shell," Zoey countered.

"A lot, then," Elise hedged, and for that, she was grateful. She did feel different now than when she'd first met him, more open to possibilities…more *real.*

Hazel nibbled her lip, the way she always did when she had heavy thoughts on her mind. "Okay, I'm just going to throw this out there," she said. "Isn't that really good? That he's gotten you to open up? Obviously, he cares about you. He called for us to come be with you."

Elise considered, glancing down at her hands she couldn't stop fiddling in her lap and then shrugged. "Maybe, but where does that leave me? I can't…" She drew in a deep breath and then admitted things she never would have before —weak things. "I feel really fragile right now. Like, if I let him in and if he crushed me, I'm not sure what I'd do after that."

"Which is really scary," Hazel offered.

Elise nodded, swallowing the emotion stuck in her throat. "It's too scary. And right now, I can't do scary. So, while it's been amazing with Archer and I feel like there is something special there, he's not ready. And I'm not ready to be hurt. It's too risky."

Zoey's expression pinched before she offered, "But what if that risk is worth it in the end?"

"But what it if isn't?" Elise countered.

Silence descended, a heavy silence of a thousand unknowns. Until Elise's cell phone beeped. She snatched it up quickly. Disappointment settled in when she saw the message was from Penny. SHIT IS GOING DOWN. GET HERE.

PRONTO. "It's Penny," she said. "I need to go." She smiled at Zoey and Hazel. "Thanks again for checking in. Love you both."

"We love you back," Zoey said.

Hazel nodded. "We sure do."

After another group hug and feeling grateful she had such good friends, Elise hopped on the subway and made her way to Penny's. She got there quickly, and Penny buzzed her in.

The moment Penny saw Elise, she frowned. "No boy toy again?"

"There is no more boy toy," Elise explained, hoping that would put the matter to rest.

"That makes no sense," Penny grumbled. "You've seemed so happy."

"Sometimes you're just better off as friends, and this is one of those times," Elise said, lying through her damn teeth. Penny's knowing look declared she read right through her. She grabbed the swivel chair and dropped into it. Not wanting to talk about it, she gestured to the monitors. "What do you have for me?"

Penny looked a moment away from arguing, but then gave in and moved along, turning back to her monitors. "Well, I thought you'd like to know I've caught something on the bug." A sly smile crossed her face as she typed on her keyboard. "Tonight, a meeting has been arranged between Isaac, Connie, and Elijah, Connie's husband."

"Do you know what the meeting is about?" Elise asked.

"Nope," Penny reported. "It all sounded very formal."

"Let me hear it."

Penny hit enter on her keyboard and then Elise felt like she was right in the middle of their conversation. Since she couldn't hear water running in the kitchen or anyone cooking or blankets shifting in the bedroom, she surmised they were likely sitting in the living room.

"I called Elijah and set up a meeting for this evening."

The voice belonged to Isaac.

"Good." A feminine voice. Connie.

Elise asked Penny, "Is it just the two of them in there?"

"Sure is," Penny replied.

Elise tilted her ear back to the conversation coming through the computer speakers. Isaac said, "Everything we've worked for is almost here, love."

"I know."

Sucking sounds followed.

"Nothing like sucking face with your brother's wife, huh?" Penny mused.

"It's gross," Elise grumbled. "And obviously, they've got some plan."

"Yeah, just wait. It's coming up."

Long minutes passed as Connie and Isaac treated themselves to each other. When they finally stopped kissing, Connie said, "Do you think Elijah knows we're the ones who have been blackmailing him?"

"Pause that," Elise said.

Penny laughed. "Thought you might be interested in that part."

"Yeah, I am," Elise said, letting that bit sink in. "They're blackmailing her husband, his brother? What the hell is wrong with these people?"

"You know what's wrong with people," Penny said harshly. "Money. Power. And revenge. That's what it's always about."

"Yeah, but to do that to your brother? Your husband?" Elise slowly shook her head, suddenly really glad Archer and Rhys had hired her on for this case. Perhaps because of her father and what he'd done, she always felt obligated to find the bad people in the world and weed them out. And she wanted these two horrible human beings exposed. "Okay, keep playing."

"No," Isaac said. "That idiot has no idea."

Elise nearly emptied her stomach all over Penny's computers at their laughter.

Connie asked, "When will he be there?"

"Seven o'clock," Isaac replied. "Soon, this will be over and we'll have everything we ever wanted."

"We will, my darling."

Penny clicked a button, and the audio ended. "They fuck next. I'm guessing you don't want to hear that."

"No, I don't," Elise said. Her stomach couldn't handle much more. She pondered all this then blew out a long breath. "Why and how are they blackmailing him? Like, for what reason?"

Penny shrugged. "I'm guessing we'll find that out when they have their little meeting tonight."

"These people are horrible human beings," Elise stated.

"Damn right, they are." Penny nodded, pushing away her keyboard. "What's the plan?"

Elise cringed. Doing the very thing she didn't want to do right now. Feeling barely able to control her emotions, she grabbed her phone from her purse and texted Archer. I KNOW THERE'S BEEN TROUBLE AT THE CLUB. BUT CAN WE MEET TONIGHT? I'VE GOT A BIG UPDATE ON THE CASE.

It felt like forever before his reply came in. YES. SHOULD RHYS BE THERE?

YES. Soon, this case would be concluded. Rhys should be there for that, too.

WHAT TIME?

The meeting between the trio was at seven o'clock. She needed time to record that conversation too. 9 O'CLOCK?

CAN I SEE YOU BEFORE THEN?

Her heart squeezed. I CAN'T. WORKING THE CASE.

See you later, then, Elise.

She could almost hear his tone of voice. He had more to say, and he planned to say it. "Okay," she said, telling said heart to pull it together. "How about I grab us some dinner while we wait for this meeting to begin? Indian sound good?"

Penny rubbed her belly. "Sounds delicious."

Elise made it a foot away before Penny called, "Hey, Elise." She turned back to Penny, who added, "Are you sure you're okay?"

She and Penny had formed an unusual friendship. It wasn't the familiar type of friendship she had with Hazel and Zoey, where she shared her daily updates, her struggles, and her joy. But this type of friendship came from respect, and deep down, Penny probably knew Elise just as well as Zoey and Hazel. She'd seen it all. The crime scene photos. The police report. The hard truths. And she didn't pity Elise. Because of that, sharing the truth came easy. "No, I don't think I am."

15

*A*rcher could barely contain himself as he sat on a stool at the bar, watching Elise approach him, exactly like she had at the beginning of the case. Only this time, everything was different. *He* was a different man. One who wasn't looking for a casual fuck. But he knew Elise would want to finish the job before he demanded her time—they were alike that way, understood the value of a job well done—so he drew on his training to stay calm and patient while Rhys handed Elise the rectangular piece of paper. "For a job well done."

She looked down at the check Archer knew was in the amount of two hundred and seventy thousand dollars. "I know I'm good," she said to Rhys, lifting her tired eyes. "But I'm not *that* good."

Rhys polished off his shot and laughed softly. "I suspect the member who paid for your show the night you were here would disagree with you."

"Oh." She blinked. "This money is for the show?"

"In part," Rhys said. "I added on the payment for the case. If I owe more, feel free to bill me."

"Ah, I think this covers it," she said with a snort. She handed it back to him. "Thanks, but I don't want the money. Cut me a new check with the payment for the case only."

As Archer knew he would, Rhys rose and refused to take it. "Do what you want with the money, Elise, but that's your money, not mine." Clearly done with the conversation, he turned away. "I've got no doubt you've got news, so let's get to it." Leaving his empty glass, he strode off.

It took all of Archer's strength not to take Elise into his arms and tell her everything was going to be all right, but he could tell by the coldness in her eyes that would never be enough. And he needed more than a few minutes to get right what he got so wrong. "Ready?" he asked her.

She gave a firm nod. "Always."

He gestured for her to follow Rhys, and he stepped in behind her as they all went into Archer's office, where Hunt and Kieran were waiting. Elise set her laptop on the desk and powered it up. Once ready, she turned back to Rhys. "Ready to hear what I found?"

Archer realized that whenever Elise spoke about her job, she never mentioned *we*, always protecting Penny. He really loved that about her. So damn loyal, so damn good.

Sitting in the opposite chair from Archer, Rhys nodded. "Yes, play it."

Elise clicked her mouse once, pulling up an audio file. "You'll hear three voices. Isaac, Connie, and the angry voice is Elijah, Connie's husband and brother of Isaac. I've only taken the one clip since it's most important. But I've got the rest for you to listen to, if you'd like."

"Got it," Rhys said.

She clicked enter, and voices soon filled Rhys' office.

Archer recognized them immediately, except for Elijah's since they'd never met, but the anger in his voice was palpable.

"Let me get this straight," Elijah ground out. "This photograph is of you, my *wife,* and my *brother,* at a sex club. You've already sold it, and it has been printed. And if I don't agree to whatever the fuck you want, you're going to reveal yourselves to the public to ruin me?"

Isaac practically purred. "Good. You understand."

A long pause. "How the fuck would this ruin me? You'll be trashing your own names."

"You've worked for years to get the nomination to become a U.S. Attorney," Connie said coolly. "You're almost there. It's in your reach. Are you really ready to walk away from that?"

"You fucking bitch," Elijah roared.

"Don't speak to her like that," Isaac growled. "Not ever, brother."

Elijah snarled. "We are not brothers. You are dead to me."

"Just give us what we want, Elijah," Connie said sweetly, softly. "And we'll leave you alone. We can quietly divorce after your appointment, and you can move on with your life."

"And *what* exactly do you want, Connie?" Elijah sneered.

A pause. "I want you to break the prenup."

Another pause. Longer this time. Until Elijah erupted. "You motherfucker." A loud bang followed by yelling that became nearly deafening.

Elise hit enter, and the audio went dead. She said to Rhys, "They break out into a fight, but I caught most of what they were saying. So, basically, when Elijah and Isaac's father died, his multimillions were left to Elijah, not Isaac, because of Isaacs's gambling addiction. Isaac was left a few million when his grandfather passed, so he's definitely not hurting for money."

"All right…" Rhys said.

Hunt and Kieran leaned forward, all eyes on Elise. Archer couldn't take his eyes off her either. He'd seen grown men look intimated surrounded by this group. Not Elise. She looked...*perfect.*

She shut her laptop, then leaned against the desk, folding her arms. "When Isaac was in rehab, he and Connie hashed out a plan to get Isaac's share of the money. So, Connie seduced Elijah and became his wife. And they waited... waited until Elijah had something he wanted bad enough that he'd give up the money to keep it. Becoming a U.S. Attorney is a lifelong dream for him, from what I understand. To be exposed like this would tarnish his image forever. His wife screwing his brother in a sex club, it's a scandal he wouldn't recover from. And no one would back his nomination."

"Jesus Christ," Hunt growled.

Kieran nodded and blew out a long breath. "Those are some money-hungry evil people right there."

Elise nodded. "Definitely." To Rhys, she added, "But there's your motive. It never had anything to do with the club. You're safe here."

"That's a relief," Rhys said to Elise. "This is good work you've done."

"Thank you," she said, offering him a genuine smile.

Look at me, Elise. Fucking look at me. Archer shifted in his chair, nearly unable to take it. Wanting this conversation to end, he said to Rhys, "Let's bring in Elijah, Connie, and Isaac. We'll give Elijah the recording to do with what he wants, and we'll terminate Connie's and Isaac's memberships."

Ire burned in Rhys' eyes. "Yes, good idea." His friend hesitated and tapped his fingers against the arm of the chair. "Shall we reopen tomorrow night?"

Archer nodded. "My team is ready."

"Excellent." Rhys smiled easily, in a way he hadn't done since all this began. He rose and clapped Archer on the shoulder. "Good work, as always."

The remainder of the tension from the breach faded from Archer's chest. He nodded his thanks before setting his attention back on Elise, who avoided his gaze. He waited for the others to all say their goodbyes and for his office to clear. Once it did, Archer let out a rough breath. Elise looked up then, and she did what he'd expected; she went to leave.

"Elise."

She stopped dead and looked at him.

He shut the door, then went to her. "I need to say something to you," he said, taking her hand when he reached her.

Tears prickled her eyes. "What do you need to say?"

He knew exactly what she needed from him, and he wouldn't fuck up again. "I love you."

She blinked. Again. And again. "I was not expecting you to stay that."

He chuckled softly, sliding his fingers between hers, never wanting to let go. "I admit I was a bit slow to that realization, and I'm sorry if you thought you weren't important enough for me to tell my friends about how our relationship had evolved. You are important. I should have seen what you needed from me."

Her gaze remained glued to him as she hung to his every word. He knew how carefully he needed to tread. One wrong move, and this would all be over. "What do you think I need?" she asked with a rough voice.

Desperate to get closer, he cupped her face. "You need for me to tell you I'm in this, Elise. All the way. That we're together. That you are my girlfriend, the only woman I want in my life." He seemed to render her speechless, so he pressed on. "What happened to you when you were little, I wish I was there to stop it. To take all that way. But at the same time, I'm amazed by you. How brave you were, even when you were so little. It's amazing that you are the woman you are today." He brushed his thumbs across her warm cheeks, knowing she was the end of the line for him. "But there's nothing to fear anymore."

"There's always something to fear," she said softly.

He gathered her hands in his and placed them on his chest. "Not here. Never here."

Tears welled in her eyes. She swallowed deeply before she said, "But what about Phoenix, your life there? I'm just not—"

"You don't need to be anything but yourself," he said firmly. "Besides, I think we've proven many times over that sex for us is *hot*, regardless if it's in front of others or not. I have not missed my nights at Phoenix, not at any point since we began."

Her brows furrowed. "You won't miss that…excitement?"

"You're exciting enough." And yet, he remembered the mansion. "There are always opportunities to watch and play in private." She nibbled her lip, and at that, he smiled, "You enjoy that, whether you want to admit it or not."

A sweet smile crossed her face. A shy one, even. Quite unlike her. "Okay, so I don't hate watching others and maybe get excited from that."

He stroked her cheeks. "We'll make this work, however we need to. Whatever you want, we do. Whatever you don't, we don't."

She hesitated, and he saw all the pieces being put together in her mind. He saw her shove away the fear and welcome love. He saw she trusted him, and he'd never been more relieved in his life. Warmth seeped into her features as she wiggled against him. "I like our games."

He brushed his thumb across her bottom lip. All the things he'd like to do with that mouth. "So do I."

Her eyes searched his for a long moment before she asked, "What does this mean? We're dating now?"

It certainly didn't feel like enough. "I'm going to show you every day what it means to be loved. Truly loved. I'm going to take care of you until you can't remember what it feels like to not be taken care of." A tear escaped her eye, and he understood that tear, knowing that it came from a place that craved a soft landing. "From that very first night I touched you, I was yours."

She leaned up and smiled, getting closer yet. "And I was yours," she whispered.

*I was yours...*Those words matched with her playful smile were his undoing. The passion that had engulfed him after meeting her rose deep in his gut, taking over his senses. Hunger. Need. And something much more primal that drove him to a new type of desire, one that was much more personal. *His.*

His to pleasure.

His to make happy.

All his.

Desperate to claim her, he thrust his hands in her hair and held tight, when a knock came on his office door. "Fuck off," he growled. The knocking stopped.

No interruptions. Not now.

Not when he needed her like he needed air to breathe. He pressed against her, and her back hit the bookcase. Her eager moan followed. "I love you, Elise," he said across her lips before reaching for the button on her jeans. "All of you." He had her pants flicked open and pushed them down, alongside her panties. "Every fucking perfect inch of you, even when you outsmart me at every turn, always one damn step ahead of me."

Eyes half lidded, she bit her lip, then stopped his world from spinning as she said, "I love you, too, Archer."

He froze, the warmth of her affection slamming into him. "I had no idea how much I wanted to hear that until right now. Tell me again."

She ground herself against him, sliding her sex up and

down the length of him outside of his pants. "I love you, Archer. I do." She slid her hands across his cheeks. "I feared losing you. But I don't want to live in fear anymore, not from you. Not when you're such a good man and make me so happy. I want it to be *us*. For always." Then she kissed him without restraint, unraveling him completely.

When she eventually broke away, he stepped back, opening his pants and sending them down to his ass. When he returned to her, he captured her face again in one hand and her thigh in the other. "I want to feel all of you. May I?"

Her eyes hooded. "I get the shot. I'm safe."

"So am I." He shifted his hips, pressing the tip of his cock against the wet silkiness, and growled at the perfect feel of her.

He pressed in a little farther, easily sliding in, dropping his mouth to hers. "Say it again," he growled against her mouth.

"I love you—"

He entered her in one swift stroke and stole the words he loved right out of her mouth. The intensity he'd always felt burned between them, but this time it was sweeter. Passion dripped from her mouth into his, and he took every little bit of it until she was panting. Ready.

He shifted his hips, slow and hard, claiming what belonged to him. What he knew now had belonged to him from the day he met her. This wasn't about pleasure, not for him. This was about marking her as his. Always his. He held her tight, pressing his weight into her, thrusting hard until his deep grunts matched her moans.

Until she dug her nails into his arms and gasped, "Go faster."

"Faster, hmm?" He thrust. Hard. Teasing her. Wanting her to beg for him.

She gasped, her eyes huge. "Please. Faster."

Holding her tight to him, he slowly withdrew, her inner walls squeezing, begging for him to return. "Before, I would have loved to win this game between us," he told her, pumping his hips light and slow as she trembled in his arms. "Now I only want you to win." Pinning her to the bookcase, he unleashed himself into hard-and-fast thrusts that had her eyes growing wide and her breath vanishing.

Until she screamed her climax, breaking apart around him, and only when she got all she needed from him did he follow her.

16

"The donation you made was very generous," Sharon, a therapist at HappyHouse, a safe haven for abused women and their children, said to Elise a few days later.

"I'm happy to do it," Elise answered honestly. She'd wondered what to do with the money from the show at Phoenix. It had felt wrong to keep it, but she didn't want to simply rip up the check either. So she took out twenty thousand for the Phoenix case, giving Penny half and depositing the other half into her bank account. After that, she'd done some research to find the best place to donate the money, and now, looking around at the kids smiling and playing with toys in this place where life wasn't full of rage and violence, she knew this was exactly where the money needed to go.

"Here, come, let me show you where your money will go," Sharon said. Elise followed down the hallway, and Sharon explained, "In this wing, we've got rooms set up for the mothers and their children. But as you can see, we're short on bunk beds for mothers who have more than one child."

The tour continued, and Elise learned about all the things the money would help support, and something broken inside her heart healed. She couldn't change the past, but she'd made good on the future. And *this,* this would have made her mother very happy.

By the time Sharon finished, Elise felt lit up inside. She returned the hug Sharon offered her and said, "Can I come by sometimes to volunteer?"

"We'd love that." Sharon smiled. "Anytime. Just call before you'd like to come."

Elise hadn't expected her night at Phoenix to help her as much as it would help others, but as she said her goodbyes to Sharon, she felt...*light.* That a heavy burden she didn't know had been there was gone now. Zoey had once told her that Phoenix was life changing, and Elise realized she was right. It had changed the course of her life forever, making things better, stronger, happier.

When she left Sharon behind and went outside, she spotted Archer leaning against his truck, and her breath caught at his smile.

She stepped into his waiting arms, and he kissed the top of her head. "Everything go well?" he asked.

"So well." She slid her arms around his back, the move feeling so natural now, like she'd always embraced him just like this. "It felt exactly right. That money is going to go a long way here."

When he leaned away, he was smiling at her. "You've done a good thing."

She nodded and smiled in return. "All I keep thinking is how good of a place this would have been for my mom." Where there was once deep pain, there was only a sad, dull ache that her mother had missed out on so much of her life.

Archer gave a slow nod of understanding. "It's good the city has this."

"It is."

He dipped his chin and gave her a slow, easy kiss before he asked, "Can I take you somewhere?"

"Always."

He had the passenger door open for her, and soon they were on their way, staying quiet on the drive into the Brooklyn Heights area. "Please tell me you don't have another case for me," she asked with a laugh, not knowing anyone in his neighborhood. "I need a little break from Phoenix business."

He chuckled. "It's not a case."

She noted a playful sparkle in his eye before he pulled up to an elegant pre-civil war brownstone row house. A wrought-iron railing and fence surrounded the front, with mature trees lining the sidewalk. She exited the truck, pretty sure this house, or one similar, featured in a movie once, but she couldn't place the movie.

"What do you think?"

She glanced sideways, finding Archer with his hands stuffed into his pockets. "What do I think of what?"

He gestured to the building. "I bought it."

"You bought this house?"

He nodded. "Yesterday, and my apartment will be going on the market in a few days." He took her hand, tugging her forward, striding up the stairs, and opening the door a moment later.

She went in first, gobsmacked at the gorgeous foyer with the glistening hardwood floors that led to a curved staircase and a sitting room on the right with an old white brick fireplace. "Holy, wow, it's gorgeous." She turned back to him, catching his sheepish smile. "You never said you were looking to move."

He gave an easy shrug. "When it's time, it's time."

"I guess you're right," she said, making her way to the

staircase and running her hand up the smooth, shiny railing. "It's absolutely stunning."

"I'm happy you think so, because I'd like you to live here with me."

Surprised, she smiled at the warmth in Archer's voice and turned around, only to find him on one knee, a little black box in his hand with a sparkling oval diamond ring inside. Feeling like her soul began to leave her body in shock, she met Archer's emotion-packed eyes.

"You don't need to say yes now." He hesitated and then gave a soft smile. "I know this is fast. You don't even have to wear the ring. But this is where I'm at, madly and hopelessly in love with you, and I want you to know it. I want us to end up here. Together. With you as my wife, and down the road, our children running up and down those stairs behind you."

Time stopped.

She forced her feet to move, and while she felt the tingle of unease that happy things couldn't possibly last, she pushed it aside. Loving Archer was the easiest thing she'd ever done in her life. She didn't want to fight happiness anymore; she wanted to welcome it. "You're right. This is where we end up. Together." She lifted her hand, holding it out to him, and laugh-cried at the surprise on his face.

"You'll marry me?" he asked, his voice rough.

"Yes, Archer, I will." He slid the ring into place, then had her in his arms a second later, spinning her around, and laughter she hoped would stay in this house filled the foyer.

"So this must be her."

Still in Archer's arms, he turned her, and she faced a slender woman with mid-length brown hair that turned up a little at the ends. Elise would recognize her eyes anywhere; they were the exact same color as Archer's. He finally set Elise down, a warm, affectionate smile crossing his face. "Elise, this is my mother, Rose."

"Hi," Elise said, quickly offering her hand. "It's really nice to meet you."

Rose smiled sweetly and moved in for a hug. The type of hug that seemed to go on and on and only got better as the seconds went by. "It's very nice to meet you, too." Her sparkling eyes met Archer's. "Especially since you make my son so happy. Did I just hear a proposal?"

Wrapping Elise in his arms from behind, he kissed the top of her head. "She said yes."

Tears welled in Rose's eyes. "How wonderful!" She called over her shoulder, "Gerry, hurry. Archer's engaged."

Gerry, a man with kind brown eyes and stylish gray hair, hurried up the porch steps. "No kidding? Great news!" He took Archer into a rough, masculine hug and then offered Elise a much gentler one. "Welcome to the family, Elise."

"Thank you."

Rose entered the foyer, taking a look around. "I take it then that this will be your new house?"

Archer nodded and then said to Elise, "I asked them to come see the place and meet you. I just wasn't expecting them so soon."

"Oh, hush," his mother snapped at him. "I was excited to see you and couldn't wait."

"Hence the running up the steps and leaving me in the wind," Gerry said with a wink to his wife.

Rose waved him off. "Don't even listen to them, Elise," she said, sliding her arm in hers. "Why don't you show me your new house while you tell me more about yourself."

"She hasn't even seen the house herself," Archer called.

"Well, then, we'll see it for the first time together," Rose said, and Elise stepped into stride with her as they headed down the hallway. "In this family, you need to make your voice heard. The men can be loud."

Archer snorted from behind them. "Elise is the loudest one of them all."

Rose chuckled and patted Elise's arm. "Good. We're going to get all alone just fine, then."

Elise just smiled at Rose's spunky attitude. And as she glanced back over her shoulder, she smiled at the warm love on Archer's expression and at all the happy possibilities ahead of them.

EPILOGUE

Three weeks later...

*E*lise placed a box of her stuff in the back seat of Archer's truck before slamming the door closed. When she went back inside the loft, she found Hazel sitting on the chair, staring down at her toes. A classic Hazel move when she was worried. She always stayed deep in her head. Elise shut the door behind her, and Hazel still didn't move. "Why do you look so sad?" she asked, taking a seat on the coffee table.

"Not sad," Hazel said, snapping her head up with a big fake smile. "I'm really happy for you and Archer."

"Hazel."

Hazel's shoulders curled, and she sighed. "I don't want to tell you, because I don't want you to worry."

"I won't worry," Elise lied breezily. She might, depending on what Hazel said next. "I'm a PI, remember? I can help you figure out anything. Get anything solved."

"I can't afford the loft on my own," Hazel said softly. "And I've decided I need to give it up, but I have no idea where I'm going to go."

Elise reached out for Hazel's hand. "You told me you'd be fine if I moved out. Why didn't you take me up on my offer to stay until you found another roommate?"

"You can't live with me forever," Hazel said with a snort. "It's okay. I'll find something else. Maybe you can help me find a place."

Her heart reached for Hazel. Out of all of them, Hazel surely thought she'd get married first. She wanted the husband, the kids, all that, but life never seemed to work out for her that way. "Okay, when do we need to do that?"

"Tomorrow."

Elise felt her eyebrows go sky high. "Tomorrow? *What?*"

Hazel cringed. "I know it's bad. But when I told Mr. Wood"—the landlord of the building—"he asked if I could leave early because he had someone interested, and I said yes."

Elise wanted to shake Hazel. "Why did you say yes if you don't have another place?"

"I felt bad," Hazel said with a small voice. "Besides, Zoey said I can stay with her until I figure out what to do next."

"Why are you staying with Zoey?"

Elise glanced back, finding Kieran behind them with a box in his hands. Obviously, he'd come from Elise's bedroom. A quick look back at Hazel revealed her pinkish cheeks. Elise fought her smile. Hazel had a real thing for Kieran. A big, bad thing. Kieran seemed to simply like teasing her. The two of them were so opposite, Elise couldn't ever picture them together, but maybe…

"Oh, it's nothing," Hazel said, breaking the silence. "Just thinking about staying with her for a bit."

Kieran frowned and set the box down on the ground. "Can't be nothing if you look that sad."

Hazel huffed and threw up her arms. "Do I really look that sad?"

"Yes," Elise and Kieran said in unison.

Hazel rolled her eyes, then reached for her cola—her absolute favorite drink. She took a long sip from her straw before she said to Kieran, "I need to move out tomorrow, and I'm not really sure where I'm going to go."

A pause.

"My place," Kieran said with a smile.

Hazel's eyes went huge. Elise was pretty sure hers did too.

Kieran chuckled at their silence. "I'm not sure why that's such a surprising idea. I've got an extra room and a basement to store your stuff. Use it. Get back on track and figure things out."

Elise looked at Hazel, finding those cheeks were now bright red. Yeah, she was crushing so hard on Kieran, even if she had yet to admit it.

"You do not have to do that," Hazel blurted out.

"What doesn't he have to do?"

Elise smiled at Archer's warm voice. He set a box down on top of Kieran's and then wrapped his arms around her from behind and dropped a kiss on her neck. Elise explained, "Hazel needs to move out of the loft by tomorrow because she's way too nice and always thinking about everyone else and not herself. Kieran offered his guest room up for her to stay in until she gets things figured out."

"Ah," Archer said, giving Hazel a quick smile. "Do you need help moving? I can bring some of my security guys over."

Hazel blinked. "Um…"

"Yeah, good idea," Kieran said. "I'm sure a few guys from the station will help too. We'll get your stuff packed up quickly and get you moved in." He gestured toward the door. "Come on. I'll take you to get some boxes, if you'd like."

Hazel finally blinked again. She swallowed. Deeply. "Are you sure?"

Kieran offered a smile that didn't look so sweet and innocent. "Of course. You're a friend. I'm glad to help out."

Watching him closely, Hazel nibbled her lip, but ultimately realized she'd run out of options. Some of the color in her cheeks faded. "Thank you so much, Kieran. That's really nice of you. I promise I won't be there long, just until I find a new place."

He winked at her. A devilish wink. "It's fine, Hazel. Really. I like your company."

Elise fought her smile as Hazel all but melted into a puddle on the floor before she found her legs and followed Kieran to the front door.

Another soft kiss on her neck had Elise turning around to face Archer. She slid her arms around his neck. "Hi."

"Hi." He kissed her, a long, slow kiss that left her wanting more. But he eventually broke away and smiled. "She'll be okay with Kieran. He's a good guy."

"Oh, I know," she said. "I just hope Hazel doesn't die from lust."

Archer chuckled. "Trust me, Kieran won't let her die. He might get her close, but he'll bring her back from the brink."

She laughed, then glanced around the living room before meeting his gaze again. "Would you ever have believed when I took that case this is where we'd end up?"

"Not in a million years," he said with a wink. "But I should have known better."

She pressed herself into his warm strength. "Why is that?"

"Because, from the very first day I learned your name after you hacked into my security, you were unforgettable."

"I was always a step ahead of you, and that's what you couldn't forget," she said, smiling up at him.

"You were," he said simply. "That's exactly what made you stand out." He lowered his arms to take her hand. "Ready to be a step ahead of me for the rest of my life?"

She laughed, free and easy, feeling her mom smiling down on her. "Definitely."

Thank you for reading!

CLICK HERE TO SUBSCRIBE TO MY MAILING LIST TO NEVER MISS A NEW RELEASE & YOU'LL GET A FREE READ TOO!

ABOUT THE AUTHOR

Stacey Kennedy is a *USA Today* bestselling author who writes contemporary romances full of heat, heart, and happily ever afters. With over 50 titles published, her books have hit Amazon, B&N, and Apple Books bestseller lists.

Stacey lives with her husband and two children in south-western Ontario—in a city that's just as charming as any of the small towns she creates. Most days, you'll find her enjoying the outdoors with her family or venturing into the forest with her horse, Priya. Stacey's just as happy curled up indoors, where she writes surrounded by her lazy dogs. She believes that sexy books about hot cowboys or alpha heroes can fix any bad day. But wine and chocolate help too.

ACKNOWLEDGMENTS

To my husband, my children, family, friends, and bestie, it's easy to write about love when there is so much love around me. Big thanks to my readers for your understanding when this book had to be pushed back because of the loss of my father – I appreciate all your kindness more than you could ever know; my editor, Lexi, for making my stories shine and for your extra patience where it came to changing my schedule; my agent, Jessica, for always having my back; my cover artist, Regina, who never ceases to amaze me with her beautiful work; my PR company, Social Butterfly, I'd be lost without you; Shayla Black and Angel Payne, my sprinting buddies, who keep me focused and for their endless advice and support. Thank you.

READ THE NEXT BOOK IN STACEY
KENNEDY'S PHOENIX SERIES:

SAVE ME

CHAPTER 1

Seated at the breakfast bar in his kitchen, Kieran Black sipped his piping hot coffee and began to understand the meaning of the saying: *no good deed goes unpunished.* His roommate of three days, Hazel Rose, stretched on tiptoe to reach a bowl on the middle shelf in the cupboard. The hem of her already short tank top rode up, revealing a trim waist his fingers twitched to grab. Her fair skin, speckled with freckles, made his mouth water and his groin tighten with a need that had been slowly killing him for the past three days.

Hell. That's what this was, and he'd placed himself right into the depths of it.

But when he saw Hazel's light blue eyes reveal her fear and loneliness, he couldn't help himself. He'd felt bad for her then. He still felt bad now, but he hadn't realized the depth of his desire for her until they were forced into close proximity.

Hindsight was a bitch.

Over the short time he'd spent with her, he discovered Hazel was good, sweet, nurturing, sexy, everything a man would want if he was looking for a wife. All the things Kieran *shouldn't* want. Ever since his parents' nasty divorce where they used him as a tool to punish each other, he'd sworn he'd never hurt another person like his parents hurt each other. From what he'd learned of Hazel over the last year, she barely dated, she didn't do one-night stands, and he doubted she'd ever let go of herself. Hazel was, with her sweet and romantic heart, the wrong woman for him. And yet . . . *and yet* . . . when she stretched up farther, her shorts inching higher, revealing enough of her incredible ass to make him rock-hard, he'd gladly offer up his left leg for a night with her.

When she reached even higher, he shot up from his seat. "I got that." She whirled around with a gasp, and as he met Hazel's pretty, wide eyes, he realized he'd yelled at her. He chuckled, though even to him he sounded tense. "You're going to hurt herself," he told her gently.

"You're probably right." She moved away with a laugh that warmed his chest, letting him reach for the bowl. "Thanks," she said when he handed it to her.

"No problem." He returned to the stool behind the island and sipped his coffee again, concerned that he was growing too used to waking up to her already in the kitchen getting ready for her day. Desperate to get his mind on something other than bending her over the counter and riding her hard, he asked, "What's your plan for today?"

"Just work." She added some yogurt, raspberries and granola to her bowl before she met him at the island. "My editor's in a mood lately, and that means we all have to work a little bit harder."

"Sounds fun."

"It's not." She leaned a hip against the island, using her spoon to scoop up yogurt. "What's your day looking like?"

"Going for a run this morning." Not only to train for the upcoming Ironman competition, but to burn off the desire simmering in his blood. "Groceries and some errands later. Tonight, I'll be hitting up Phoenix."

"Oh, cool," she said, a blush creeping across her cheeks at the mention of the exclusive sex club that catered to the rich and famous of New York City.

He held back his grin. Never in all his twenty-nine years had he ever met anyone as innocent as Hazel. His whole adult life, he'd surrounded himself with passionate people who loved sex, the dirtier the better. He'd been involved in sex clubs and private play parties since his first week of college. Those parties that catered to the elite of New York City society was where he eventually met Rhys, the owner of Phoenix, where he'd been a member since Rhys opened the club. He had developed a strong friendship with Rhys and Archer, head of security for Phoenix. Kieran rarely spoke to his parents now, by choice, to keep their drama out of his life, but he'd found a chosen family in his friends, and he'd walk through flames for any of them.

"What are you doing tonight?" he asked.

She leaned over the island, crossing her arms, revealing more than enough cleavage. Kieran breathed past the squeezing of his chest. He'd swear she was doing this on purpose to taunt him, but Hazel didn't have that type of manipulation in her. She blushed at even the slight hint of attention; she couldn't pull off something like this. "Going to look at a few more places with Elise."

"Like I said before, there really is no rush," he said, and she glanced up at him through long lashes. "It's nice having the company."

"Thanks, but I really don't want to overstay my welcome."

He was about to reply that she could never do that, but a knock on the door had Hazel scooting away like a rabbit running from a fox. She opened the door a moment later, and Kieran's lifelong friend Hunt Walker strode in. He took in the scene, his light brown eyes scanning the room, something he did even before he became a cop with the NYPD. His golden-brown hair was hidden beneath a Yankees baseball cap. He wore long basketball shorts, a muscle tank top and sneakers. While Hunt didn't swim or bike, he always came on Kieran's runs when he trained. After he took in Hazel, his gaze cut to Kieran and Hunt's brow furrowed slightly. Hunt never missed much.

Kieran shook his head and moved to the sink. He dumped the rest of his coffee out and put the mug in the dishwasher. When he reached Hazel by the door, he said, "Let me know if you need me to go with you to look at any of the places."

"No way," she said. "You're even pickier than Elise."

He'd gone to see one place with her yesterday. "Yeah, 'cause it was shit," he stated. "You deserve better than that, Hazel."

Her cheeks turned a darker shade of red.

Hunt observed the situation like a cop, studying every movement while Kieran slipped into his running shoes, lacing them up.

"See you later, Hazel," Hunt called.

"Bye," she said with a wave. Her gaze fell to Kieran and held.

Kieran swore she looked at him like she wanted him to come and kiss her goodbye. He bit back the urge to take her into his arms and his bedroom, and stepped out into the quiet, sunny morning.

He lived in the Upper East Side. His Victorian brownstone was among the assortment of buildings with old-world charm in every direction. He'd inherited the property from his late paternal grandfather, who was the only reason Kieran wasn't a total screwup. His parents divorced when Kieran was twelve, and his grandfather helped him weather their rage, having Kieran stay with him often. Instead of leaving his inheritance to Kieran's father, he left it all to Kieran, and his own relationship with his father never recovered. But Kieran had loved his grandfather, and he appreciated the leg up the money offered him.

"Want to tell me what that was all about?" Hunt asked, sidling up next to Kieran at the bottom of the porch steps.

"Nope." Kieran shut out the world, focusing on his stretching routine, getting his muscles loose and limber for the run.

When he finished up with his final calf stretch, Hunt raised his eyebrows. "Are you sure you've got nothing on your mind?"

"Just ready to run," Kieran said, not even sure he could formulate clear sentences. He took off running at full speed, letting his emotions fuel his workout. The first ten minutes were painful, each step burning, both his legs and his lungs crying out for him to stop, until he fell into a steady rhythm and his body felt lighter, his steps easier.

When they reached the East River, running along the paved pathway, Hunt yelled from behind him, "Fuck, man. Slow the hell down."

Kieran glanced back over his shoulder, barely registering the pain he endured. But one look at the way Hunt wobbled, he realized he'd been going hard. Hunt trained in the gym and had the thick physique to show for it. Kieran was lean from long runs, swims and bike rides, he'd always been faster on his feet. He slowed until he was walking and then headed back toward Hunt. "Sorry," he said, swiping at the sweat on his forehead with his arm.

Hunt was bent over, desperately attempting to catch his breath, his face cherry-red. "What in the hell are you running from?" he asked.

Kieran glanced away to the water. "You know what I'm running from."

A pause. When Kieran met Hunt's gaze again, his brow was furrowed. "Hazel?"

Kieran moved to the railing, leaning over it, relishing the coolness of the metal beneath his arms. "I shouldn't have asked her to live with me. Biggest mistake I've ever made."

Hunt settled in next to him, breathless. "Why, what's she done?"

"It's not what she's done," Kieran stated. "It's what I'm going to do if I don't get her out of my place." Her sugary scent … her luscious body … he was damn tired of bringing himself to completion with her on his mind, instead of tasting her for himself.

Hunt's mouth twitched. "Ah, I see. A little tempting treat is taunting you?"

"Taunting isn't the right word, she's not doing anything." Kieran tapped a finger against his head. "She's in here. All the fucking time."

Hunt looked out to the water, so Kieran did the same. "Is it so bad that she's in your head?" Hunt asked a few minutes later. "She's single. You're single."

"Yes, it's bad." Kieran had thought this through from every angle. "Hazel is a romantic. You know that. You've heard her talk with Elise and Zoey. She wants marriage, a family, that type of life. And that's not the life I want."

"Who's to say that's what Hazel is looking for right now?" Hunt asked, as a couple of runners jogged past them.

"Of course, that's what she wants. A sweet girl like that isn't looking for a fast fuck after a night of clubbing."

Hunt's mouth twitched again. "She is sweet, I'll give you that. But considering she's not in a long-term relationship, and hasn't been in one since we've met her, maybe there's more going on there. Maybe she's looking for something different."

If only it were that easy. Kieran sighed, looking out at the murky water again, a boat slowly making its way down the East River. "And there's the other problem. I care."

"We all care about Hazel."

"Yeah, but I'll care about how she'll feel after I take what I want," Kieran explained.

"That is a problem," Hunt said. Then he gave a half smile. "Maybe you're wanting something that you're not ready to admit to then."

"I want her in my bed, nothing more." Kieran remembered the yelling, the fights that went on for hours, the rage. He recalled the way his parents pulled and yanked at him, each one making him take sides. For years, they played horrible games. Until one day, Kieran realized there was no love in his family. And he no longer loved his parents. How could he when he no longer respected them? He never trusted love after that.

Hunt paused for a long moment. "Sounds like you've got an opportunity on your hands."

"Oh? Do tell."

"We've all seen the way Hazel blushes around you. The way she stares at you a little longer than anyone else. How she freezes when you walk into the room. She's interested. It's obvious to all of us. Why don't you find out exactly what she's interested in?"

Kieran frowned. "Yeah, and what if she wants a relationship and I hurt her?"

"You won't." The warm breeze carried the yeasty scent from the bakery behind them as Hunt dropped a hand on Kieran's shoulder. "Your nature is to save, not to hurt."

Kieran absorbed Hunt's advice, glancing back out at the rippling water. Something had to give. Ignoring his attraction to Hazel wasn't working. If anything, the lust pulsating between them was deepening. He suspected her being off-limits was what drove his insatiable need, but there was no pretending the desire didn't exist. He had to find a safe way to be with her that wouldn't break her heart.

Before he could decide on a response, his cell phone vibrated in his pocket. He took a quick look at the screen. "It's Rhys. He's asking if we can meet him at the tailor's tomorrow at seven o'clock for final measurements." Rhys's wedding was two months from now. Archer's, three weeks after Rhys's. Kieran glanced up and Hunt nodded, then he fired off a text. Hunt and I will be there. Once he slid his phone back into his pocket, he ran his hand through his sweaty hair. "Who would have ever believed a year ago we'd be attending not only Rhys's wedding, but Archer's too."

Hunt used his shirt to wipe the sweat off his forehead. "Not me, that's for damn sure."

The thought that had been haunting Kieran lately still weighed heavily on his mind. He'd lived his life one way. He'd chosen to not date seriously or go the marriage route. To not bring children into this world. To not offer love and then mess it up somehow. And yet, being around Rhys and Archer had him wavering. "Do you think we're missing out?"

"On what?"

"On having a woman in our lives."

Hunt grinned. "We have women all the time."

Kieran's skin crawled to even mention it. "We don't have what Rhys or Archer have."

"No, we don't, that's true," Hunt said in understanding. Both Rhys and Archer had been longtime bachelors before finding themselves caught up in their women's spells. "Nah, man," Hunt eventually said. "We're not missing out on shit."

A lie. After years of friendship, Kieran read right through Hunt.

Have I chosen the wrong path?

After a moment of thought, he knew he wouldn't find that answer today. Besides, right now, the bigger problem was keeping his hands *off* Hazel. A task becoming harder as the long hours went ticked by. "Come on," he said to Hunt, taking off at a run again. "Try not to fall behind this time."

"Bastard," Hunt growled.

Kieran chuckled, and he ran faster.